Rose knew that he was possibly the most handsome man ever to draw breath.

She knew that the sculpted structure of Zac's face was arresting, all fascinating angles and intriguing planes, a masterful straight nose, carved cheekbones. His sensually sculpted wide mouth and glowing golden-toned olive skin that matched the dark hair that sprang from his broad forehead and curled into his neck.

What she hadn't known was that his dark gaze, set below thick straight brows, could paralyze a person. That his sheer masculinity and the strength of his long lean body, not disguised by the perfect tailoring, could send a quiver through a person's body.

She shook her head to free herself from the sensual fog, realizing that her mouth was open, she closed it. *Wow, that was embarrassing!* she thought as she rearranged her features into one of cool polite interest.

"You wanted to see me?" She tried to direct her gaze over his left shoulder, but that hard dark stare had a mesmeric quality...no man should have eyelashes that long.

Kim Lawrence lives on a farm in Anglesey with her university-lecturer husband, assorted pets who arrived as strays and never left, and sometimes one or both of her boomerang sons. When she's not writing, she loves to be outdoors gardening or walking on one of the beaches for which the island is famous—along with being the place where Prince William and Catherine made their first home!

Books by Kim Lawrence

Harlequin Presents

A Passionate Night with the Greek
Claimed by Her Greek Boss

A Ring from a Billionaire

Waking Up in His Royal Bed
The Italian's Bride on Paper

Jet-Set Billionaires

Innocent in the Sicilian's Palazzo

Spanish Secret Heirs

The Spaniard's Surprise Love-Child
Claiming His Unknown Son

The Secret Twin Sisters

The Prince's Forbidden Cinderella

Visit the Author Profile page
at Harlequin.com for more titles.

Kïm Lawrence

—

HER FORBIDDEN
AWAKENING IN GREECE

HARLEQUIN

PRESENTS

H HARLEQUIN®
PRESENTS™

PLEASE RECYCLE

Recycling programs
for this product may
not exist in your area.

ISBN-13: 978-1-335-59283-5

Her Forbidden Awakening in Greece

Copyright © 2023 by Kim Lawrence

For questions and comments about the quality of this book,
please contact us at CustomerService@Harlequin.com.

Harlequin Enterprises ULC
22 Adelaide St. West, 41st Floor
Toronto, Ontario M5H 4E3, Canada
www.Harlequin.com

Printed in U.S.A.

HER FORBIDDEN
AWAKENING IN GREECE

CHAPTER ONE

THE MOMENT HE stepped out of the soundproofed sanctuary of his office Zac was hit by the nerve-shredding racket; the small window of silence had lulled him into a false sense of security. 'Theos!' he gritted under his breath.

It was unrelenting. How could anything so small make this much noise? he wondered as the scene of the recent handover floated through his head. There had been no noise then, the silence broken only by the voice of the woman holding the impossibly small bundle. The woman from child services had offered the child to him and Zac, who relished challenges, had frozen, his arms at his sides—a challenge too far.

The nanny had stepped into the breach, and the moment had passed. He doubted if anyone had noticed, but he had, his first test and he had failed. All he had got was a view of a mop of dark hair against the blanket the baby was bundled up in. Did he resemble his father or mother…? Zac didn't know. He hadn't entered the nursery yet…delaying the inevitable, he knew, but his feelings, his *anger*, were still raw, and what would his presence achieve?

He was determined the child, Declan, would lack nothing growing up, except of course a mother and father. Before it could settle over him he pushed the bleakness away. His energy was better spent on dealing with the present—which involved inconsolable crying and sleep deprivation. In retrospect the nanny's advice to dispense with the services of the night nurse after two nights had been proved both optimistic and premature, given the fact the baby had not stopped crying since.

Despite her assurances that the infant was not ill and this situation was *normal*, Zac had opted for a second opinion. The paediatrician of worldwide renown recommended by Zac's own physician had backed her up after his house call—turned out if there was enough cash involved *everybody* did house calls.

The medic's patronising attitude had set Zac's teeth on edge, but then experts who dumbed down always irritated him. An irritation that faded into insignificance when compared with this constant racket.

If the last few days had taught him anything it was that any effort to tune out the auditory assault of a six-week-old child who, in truth, had every right to sound unhappy, given his start in life, was pointless.

Not running away, more walking calmly, he told himself as he strode towards the blonde wood door and his private lift that gave access to the top-floor penthouse he occupied when in London.

His route through the normally soothing open-plan shades of white gleaming space involved a few detours to avoid the signs of the extra member of the household. The live-in nanny had looked at him blankly when he had pointed out the overspill of items from the nursery, then laughed and said cheerfully, 'Wait until he's walking.' As though she thought he was joking.

He hadn't been, and to be fair she appeared to have made an effort, or one of the other staff had. Even so the overspill included a stack of freshly laundered baby clothes on his favourite leather swivel chair, and rings on the previously spotless surface of a low glass-topped table. He stepped over a damp towel on the floor and clenched his teeth while trying and failing to tune out the nails-digging-into-a-chalkboard wail that had stepped up another painful ear-shattering decibel.

Zac liked order in all things. His life was compartmentalised, business and private, there was no messy overspill between the two, which was one of the more minor reasons he had decided never to have children of his own. This had not changed despite the fact one of the guest suites had been turned into a nursery and an en suite room for a nanny. This child did not carry his flawed DNA so, even with him as a parent, he had a chance.

Zac liked space and, while the London penthouse did not compare in size to his other homes,

the ten-thousand-plus square footage of the minimalist apartment at a prestigious address was large
enough to accommodate this inconvenience—at least
on paper.

It had quickly become obvious that the reality was
very different. Reality was something he was struggling with at the moment.

He still hadn't got his head around the fact that
Liam and his young wife were gone. It seemed sur-
real, and he was too busy dealing with the practi-
calities of being a guardian to a newborn to even
think about grieving. It was all he could do to keep
his anger in check.

Such a bloody waste.

If Liam had known the unspeakable, utterly impossible would happen, that he and his sweet, bub-
bly wife Emma wouldn't be around to care for their
son, he might have made a less sentimental and more
practical decision when choosing a guardian for their
first and, as it turned out, *only* child, than his friend.

But Liam always had been ruled by his heart.
The first time Zac had seen him, a student like himself, Liam had been emptying his pockets to fill the
charity collection tin that other students entering
the union bar were pretending not to notice. Zac
had stepped in when he'd found Liam counting out
coins and coming up short to pay for his beer—he'd
grinned and toasted Zac, calling him his guardian
angel.

They had still been students when Liam had become Zac's very first employee after Zac had spotted

a gap in the market and had bought his first property to lease out to well-heeled students with no cash-flow problems.

Later, when Liam had started his own IT firm, Zac had been his first customer, not because Zac was anyone's guardian angel, but because Liam had been the best at what he did. Sentiment and business did not mix and if this pragmatic approach meant people called him ruthless, he could live with it. In fact his reputation for playing hard ball frequently worked in his favour.

There had certainly been no guardian angel watching over Liam and Emma when the driver of an articulated truck had had a heart attack and swerved across the central reservation.

The entire family gone…though actually not. Their premature baby had been deemed not ready to come home from the hospital with his mother, or he too would have been snuffed out.

Zac was feet away from escaping through the door, running through the pros and cons of moving into a hotel until the baby stopped crying and try-ing not to replay those grim words—*Wait until he's walking*—when he caught the gaudy display in the periphery of his vision. He could ignore a lot, but there were limits!

He opened his mouth to call only to find the man who ran his domestic life and much else besides al-ready standing at his elbow. If Zac had believed in such things, he would have said the guy was psy-chic, but what he did believe in was efficiency. And

Arthur, ex-military, might have gained a few inches round the middle since he'd left the service, but he had not lost any of his military bearing or his un-flappable problem-solving genius.

'A moment, boss.'

Zac was distracted from his justifiable outrage when the older man proceeded to remove earplugs from his ears.

'Now why didn't I think of that? You're a genius.'

The older man gave a modest smile that tugged at the scar on his cheek but looked less than his normal buoyant self once exposed to the noise. 'A problem?'

'What are these?' Zac's finger stabbing expressed his disgust.

'Birthday cards. Many happy returns, boss.'

Zac had actually forgotten it was his birthday, and hadn't celebrated one since he was eighteen, but his extended family refused to believe this and every year the envelopes continued to arrive. The surprise parties and dinner invitations, which usu-ally involved balloons, drunken speeches and the inevitable *suitable* woman. Zac made a point of hav-ing a full diary the days either side of his birthday, or rather Arthur did.

'Are you trying to be funny?'

'No, trying to make light of a tense situation,' the other man responded, wincing slightly as another bellow permeated the room.

Zac shared his pain.

'The maid is new. She thought she was showing initiative,' he continued drily. 'I have removed the banner from the library, and the balloons your sister…?' He paused, brow crinkling.

'It doesn't matter which one,' Zac cut back quickly. The list of possibilities was long.

Sometimes it seemed endless. He found himself comparing himself to Liam, who had had no living relatives. Zac had them in abundance, he didn't lack sisters, and when you added the nieces and nephews, he sometimes struggled to match the child with the right parent. The entire tribe seemed to live in each other's pockets, and tried to pull Zac into their social circle, which had got larger as the years progressed.

His youngest half-sister was ten and his oldest stepsister twenty-nine. The oldest and several in between had children of their own from within marriages and outside. There were the partners that brought their own offspring from previous relationships: they had one divorce, one remarriage and several reconciliations between them…also a handful of affairs.

Zac steered clear of the soap opera that was their lives, not because he did not *care* for his family—he did—but they were incapable of recognising boundaries any more than a puppy was. They shared everything and he, and his inability to reciprocate, hurt them. Both sides of the equation benefited from an emotional distance.

The idea of introducing any woman who shared his bed to his family was his nightmare scenario. Bed-sharing suited Zac very well. He'd tried to explain to his family that he had no desire for a partner to share his life with but they insisted that he'd change his mind once he found the right person.

His mother had found the right person in Kairos, his stepfather, and look how well that had ended. Too young to recall the details, he remembered the yelling and rows and then, worse somehow, the utter total silence as they had moved on to the indifference phase, not an experience he ever intended to enjoy. So, yes, he was looking out for the right person so that he could cross the street to avoid her.

He was willing to concede there *were* happy marriages, but it would seem getting to that point involved kissing a lot of frogs and paying divorce lawyers through the nose.

After his parents' eventual amicable divorce after wedded disharmony, Zac's stepfather, Kairos, went on to have what was, or at least *appeared* to be, a very happy marriage and four children with his second wife. The way the volatile pair argued sometimes made him wonder if those children, who, unlike himself, were all biologically Kairos's own, were the reason the marriage had lasted.

Not that Kairos had ever treated his cuckoo in the nest any differently, but Zac always *knew* he was different—the consciousness of *how* different never left him. He had been taking a step back, keeping himself apart, all his life rather than maintain a pretence of being an integral part of this happy family.

It was an open secret, the world knew that Kairos was not his biological father, and occasionally the media speculation about who his actual father was would surface. Would some enterprising investigative journalist one day follow the breadcrumbs to the juicy truth?

He was prepared, but he knew that his mother was not. The face she presented to the world gave no hint of her vulnerability. Escaping his father to save him had been the actions of a brave woman, a proud woman. If the history became known people would see her as a victim and Zac knew that was her worst nightmare.

The full story was known only to Kairos, Zac and his mother, so no one outside realised just how generous Kairos had been in treating Zac as his own. To take on any man's child was a big thing, but the child of a father like his…that took a great man, which his stepfather was.

The Greek shipping line billionaire had been even-handed with all his children, or, as his biological children put it, mean and miserly to the people he should care for most. That was their reaction to the news that their father's intention was to leave his fortune to various charities. They would not starve but they would have to make their own way in the world as he had.

Zac took the view that it was Kairos's money, and what he did with it was his business. In a way it had been a relief. He didn't want to take any more from the generous man and no golden spoon meant no expectation, no restrictions. As there were no footsteps to follow, he could be himself, and, unlike his stepsiblings, Zac had a hunger for success.

Strictly speaking, Zac was meant to spend an equal time with both parents as he grew up, but in reality he hadn't. His mother's next three husbands had not considered his presence a plus, and Zac could see where they were coming from! Zac had hit six feet at thirteen and carried on growing. If you added his physical six feet of teenage angst to his fiercely protective attitude towards his mother, he could not have been a relaxing presence. The situation had meant he'd actually spent more time with Kairos, who moved between Greece, London and the Norwegian home that they euphemistically referred to as a cabin. The amount of time he spent with his mother and the children she had with each of her husbands was limited.

Seven half- and stepsiblings, the number of nephews and nieces growing yearly, and all of them, even those that could not write yet, sent him birthday and Christmas cards.

'Sorry, this noise is—' He took a deep breath. Even miracle-maker Arthur couldn't make a baby stop crying—could *anyone* stop this baby crying?

When the older man didn't meet his eyes, and cleared his throat, Zac knew it could not be good news. 'About the noise, boss...'

'Yes, I know, I'll speak to the nanny again...'

'The nanny has handed in her notice, a family situation apparently.'

Zac closed his eyes and counted slowly to ten...a pointless exercise as ten thousand would not solve this problem. For the first time in his life Zac could not see beyond the problem or even a way around.

Liam was gone.

'Sir?'

Zac shook his head to free himself of the statement that still didn't make sense. The funeral hadn't made it seem any more real, but it was real.

Zac had broken a leg once playing soccer and walked off the pitch. Pain was something to be conquered, but this pain was different, this pain was visceral.

After all his hard work, Liam had been living the dream, *his* dream, the IT business he'd built from scratch, the beautiful, sweet wife and the child he'd longed for, and it had all been snatched away.

And people still believed in happy endings? Continued to look for love when falling in love seemed to mean massive disillusionment or loss.

The last time he had spoken to Liam, his friend had been going to the hospital to pick up Emma.

'I told you I'd marry her, didn't I, Zac, when she walked into that bar?'

'You did indeed, and I laughed.' Because only fools and Liam believed in love at first sight.

'Em laughed too. She thought I was insane…' he had reminisced, his voice warm as he'd spoken of his wife. 'Emma doesn't want to come home without the baby, but they just need to keep your godson in a few more days. You will, won't you, be godfather, Zac?'

A card, one of the garish home-made variety, fluttered to the floor. He bent and picked it up, crushing it in his hand as he did so, pushing away the sound of his friend's voice and wondering if the time would come when he would be unable to recall it.

A bleakness settled over him as he shoved the crumpled card into his trouser pocket before gesturing to the rest. 'Just bin them, will you?'

'Certainly. The nanny...?'

'Get in touch with the agency...no, I'll do it.' It would be some compensation to let them know how low his level of satisfaction with them was.

In the underground garage, Zac had just got behind the wheel of his sleek designer car when his phone rang. He glanced at the screen ID and switched the engine back off before putting the phone on speaker.

'Have I caught you at a bad time?'

'No, it's fine, Marco.' Liam had been his first employee and Marco had been his first well...*very* well-heeled tenant back in their uni days, the only two friendships forged back then to survive the transition from student life to the real world.

'Sorry I couldn't get to the funeral. Kate—'

'Liam would have understood,' Zac cut in immediately.

Crown Prince Marco Zanetti got straight to the point, a characteristic that Zac had always approved of in the other man.

'I need your help, Zac. I know you have a lot on your plate at the moment with the baby... How is it going?'

'Work in progress.'

'If you can't or don't feel able, just say.'

'Don't worry, I will,' Zac promised drily, knowing full well that, had the situation been reversed, the Crown Prince of the island kingdom of Renzoi would do anything for him, no questions asked. Zac had few close friends, and now one less.

'So how can I help?'

Marco told him and Zac heard him out before responding.

'So Kate was adopted?' An image of his friend's beautiful new red-headed bride flashed into his head. 'She never knew she had a twin?' That must have been quite a discovery to make, he mused.

'*Identical* twin. When the marriage broke up she stayed with the father and Kate went with her mother.'

'What did they do, pull straws?' He was no father, not in the real sense, but for Zac the idea of parents dividing up a family as though they were a record collection was incomprehensible.

'I asked myself the same thing,' Marco admitted, his voice hard as he added, 'The records I have seen suggest the mother was desperate to keep both girls, but the father threatened a custody battle. The bastard admitted, boasted during our last conversation that he split them to punish their mother, told her he'd get both, prove her unfit.'

Zac swore, adding. 'But surely he wouldn't have stood a chance!'

'Probably not but she knew how convincing he

can be and could she risk losing both babies? Awful choice to make.'

'She died?'

'And he refused to take Kate back—seems she was always sniffing and crying—his words.'

Though ironically that rejection turned out to be lucky for Kate—her adoptive family are the real deal. She had a good childhood.'

'He sounds a charmer,' Zac observed sardonically, thinking there were a lot out there, including his own father.

'The guy is…' The expletive down the line drew a nod of agreement from Zac. 'He is no longer in the picture.'

Zac approved of the cold implacability in his friend's voice. Maybe Marco had not changed that much.

'So you're saying Kate wants to find her sister and you want me to locate her.' Zac's dark brows drew into a puzzled line above his deep-set dark eyes. Marco had resources at his command that few could match. He could only assume that the prince was outsourcing the search to avoid information leaks within the palace.

'Contacting her or not is Kate's call and we—or at least I—know where she is…and on paper there is nothing to suggest that she is…that she…' He hesitated.

Zak helped the other man out. 'Is like the father?' The subject of tainted genes, and the circuitous nurture versus nature debate, was one he was no stranger to, having spent his formative years watching for signs of inherited weakness, for his own tainted genes surfacing, until he'd latterly found some sort of closure.

If he was a monster in waiting, the chances were he would not notice the signs and, even if he did, what would he do about it? He was what he was, his philosophical attitude stopped short of risking passing his flawed genes on to his own children.

'The debacle with her birth father upset Kate a lot and I don't want anything like that happening again. This pregnancy is not an easy one. I just want to double-check before I give Kate the details.'

'So you want me to check her out…and what…?' Realisation hit and Zac's brow smoothed. 'Ah, you want me to pay her off if there's an issue?' Zac speculated, seeing the logic of this plan. With him acting as Marco's proxy, the other man would have deniability and clean hands if his wife found out.

'Pay her off? No, Zac, I don't want you to pay her off!'

Shock followed by outrage resounded down the line, which seemed a pretty irrational response to what was an obvious and expedient solution to this problem. The Marco he had known would have recognised this too. Marriage had changed his royal friend.

Did marriage change every man? Zac did not intend to personally test his theory.

'I don't lie to Kate.'

Except by omission, thought Zac.

'Our relationship is based on honesty.'

The fact that Marco obviously believed what he was saying deepened the cynical grooves around Zac's mouth. Some marriages worked, but *honest…*? Even marriages that were considered successful, like that of his stepfather and his beautiful, charming second wife, had their share of half-truths and compromise.

'I just want Kate to know what to expect this time, to be prepared, no nasty surprises. She's going to be mad as hell with me for waiting until after the birth,' he admitted with a laugh. 'But her blood pressure is troubling the… You don't want to know this, do you?'

Zac, who really didn't, said nothing.

'I'm prepared to take the flak if it's about keeping Kate and the baby safe.'

'If there were skeletons that your team didn't—'

'I'm not asking you to dig for dirt,' the prince shot back, and Zac could hear the frown in his voice. 'I've got dossiers but they can't tell the whole story. The father didn't have a record, he just conned his way through life. Some of that might have rubbed off on his child…'

Zac could see why Marco had decided that it was all about nurture—to take the opposing view that DNA was responsible would mean that his wife was tainted too.

'My stepfather is a saint, it didn't rub off on me, Marco.'

'Oh, you have your moments. I know that you

were the anonymous investor who bailed Liam out in the early days when he could have gone under.'

A spasm of impatience quivered across Zac's mobile lips. 'That was Liam and I knew he'd succeed. There was no risk or altruism involved.'

'Don't worry, I won't tell anyone you have a heart.'

Zac didn't hide his impatience. 'Look, Marco, I don't really see what I can find out, short of dating her, that—'

The lightness vanished from Marco's voice, leaving it cold as ice as he shot back, 'I do *not* want you to date her, Zac, you're the last man in the world that I would… That would be a game-changer for me, do you hear what I am saying?' Marco asked, drawing a very firm verbal red line in the sand.

Zac took no offence from the tone, and saw no point defending his reputation or pointing out that he had his faults, but he was no heartbreaker. He had never dated a woman who wanted more than sex, or a partner for an event, frequently both.

He wouldn't want someone like him to date a sister-in-law of his either.

'Fair enough. So what do you want me to do?'

'I want to know if she is *genuine*, that her character is… It just so happens that you are actually in the perfect position to *observe* her, Zac.'

Zac smiled a little to himself at the *'observe'* that carried the heavy message: *Look, don't touch.* Marco need not have worried. There were enough women out there without pursuing one who came with complications. 'I don't quite see how.'

'She works for you.'

The pen that Zac had been rotating through his long fingers during the conversation slipped to the car's carpeted floor. 'You sure about that?' Redheads did stand out, so if they were identical he would have remembered a twin of Kate Zanetti.

'Yes, she's a nursery nurse in one of your staff crèches. I just thought perhaps you could *observe*? Put some feelers out, see what her reputation in the workplace is. Is she reliable? You know the sort of thing—could she make Kate—'

'Unhappy?' The interruption seemed a safe bet. These days his wife's happiness seemed to be Marco's main priority. Was she his? For his friend's sake, Zac hoped so.

'Exactly, be inventive.'

'I can be inventive, certainly—nursery nurse... like a nanny, right...?' Zac said slowly.

'I suppose so.'

'Leave it to me.'

'Thanks, Zac.'

'No problem. Give my love to Kate.'

Zac ended the call, a smile on his lips as he started up the almost silent engine. Kill two birds with one stone—so long as there was no sex involved he doubted Marco would care much about his methods.

He needed childcare and Marco needed a character assessment. The two needs meshed nicely.

CHAPTER TWO

'ROSE!'

Rose, who was shrugging an oversized denim jacket on as she walked along the corridor, was tempted to pretend she hadn't heard...but her conscience refused to take a day off.

'Hi, Jac,' she said as her immediate superior in the nursery, seven months pregnant, waddled towards her. If this was about an extra shift, she'd say no, though the dark shadows under Jac's eyes did make her determination waver.

The fact was, of course, that in the end she wouldn't. Rose recognised this inability to say no as one of her character flaws, she simply couldn't, and when it came to resisting a hard-luck story she was toast.

On the plus side, extra hours meant a bigger pay packet and there was no pretending that wouldn't be useful, because she no longer had the security of her small nest egg for emergencies.

Not since Dad had turned up out of the blue saying he owed some people money and they were *serious* people.

Again, even though the story was probably fiction, she couldn't take the risk. He was her dad. When had she realised that with her dad the line between fiction and fact was blurred?

Looking into his eyes before he'd buried his face in his hands in an attitude of despair, she'd seen only utter sincerity, which meant little. He was so good at rearranging the truth that she suspected he believed his own lies most of the time—but he was her dad so she could never say no.

She'd nursed her mug of tea, he'd refused to join her, and opted for the dregs of her cooking brandy while telling her she was a good girl. She had handed over her savings knowing that, despite his promise to pay her back, she wouldn't be seeing the money again.

He might have lost a little hair, but he'd not lost *it*, she had realised, watching sadly from her window as her still handsome dad had crossed the street, his slumped shoulders squaring the farther away he got and the swagger in his step getting more pronounced.

She hadn't known whether to laugh or cry as he'd morphed into a dapper, stylishly dressed figure with a spring in his step and a cheque in his pocket. Ever the prince charming when there was someone to impress—in this instance the smartly dressed woman with long legs exiting a convertible—he gallantly offered an elderly lady his arm to cross the busy road.

The tableau had stayed with her. It encapsulated

her dad—he was never going to change, which left the option of *her* changing... It sounded so simple but changing the habit of a lifetime was not easy.

Her dad was the reason that she was never taken in by charismatic men. The more good-looking or charming they appeared, the wider the berth she gave them. It gave her an advantage over the women who had their hearts broken or their bank accounts emptied by good-looking charmers—for that she had her dad to thank.

There had always been a woman in his life. Some who had moved in with them during her childhood had been nice, others less so and Rose had been quite glad when they'd left. As she'd got older, and, some people said, quite pretty, there were more *others* who resented her presence.

Her dad didn't like friction in his home and had not put up any opposition to her decision to move into a bedsit at seventeen after giving up on the financially impractical idea of studying medicine her teachers had been encouraging. She'd set her sights instead on becoming a nursery nurse, funding herself by taking an extra job to supplement the bar work she'd already been doing.

A girl her age around the house made him feel old, her dad had admitted, joking with a wink that living with her old dad was cramping her style.

Living with her old dad, Rose mused, her lips twisting as the memory resurfaced, had meant that she didn't have a clue what her style was. She wasn't cynical enough to imagine that all men were toxic. The problem was how could you tell the difference?

A problem for another day, she thought as Jac reached her. The priority was to be firm. Say no for once in your life, Rose, she told herself with exasperation.

'Oh, Rose, I'm so glad I caught you. I'm sorry, but…the *boss* wants to see you in his office.'

Since they had yet to fill the post, the head of HR was standing in until they recruited a new manager for the crèche facilities.

'Now? Couldn't you just tell Mr Hewitt that I'm—'

'Oh, no, not him, *the* boss.'

Rose shook her head in confusion.

'Mr Adamos, *Zac* Adamos.'

Rose giggled. Jac was well known for her quirky sense of humour.

'No, *seriously*…?' Her soft gurgle of amusement morphed into a grunt of pain as she struggled to disentangle a flaming curl that had managed to wrap itself around the button on her blue shirt. 'Look, I really do have to get going, Jac,' she pushed out between clenched teeth as she performed the delicate operation.

When she succeeded in her task and looked up, Jac wasn't smiling. 'No, I am being *serious*.' Her voice lowered to an awed whisper. 'He has asked to see you, *by name*.' Her ponytail bobbed as she shook her head, her eyes wide as saucers. 'What have you done, Rose?'

The lingering faint flush across Rose's high

curved cheeks faded as she realised this was not a gotcha joke, leaving her fair skin marble pale. She pressed a hand to her throat, able to feel the vibration of her pulse.

This, whatever *this* turned out to be, could not be good and she could not afford to lose this job.

The likes of a humble nursery nurse in one of the extremely well-staffed crèches provided for staff across the offices of Adamos Inc—a perk that was not, credit where credit was due, reserved for senior management—did not get invites to the CEO's office.

That privilege or punishment, depending on your viewpoint, was reserved for employees with impressive titles that were often not self-explanatory, but basically way above her pay grade. She frowned as she frantically trawled through any recent possible transgressions that might explain this invitation.

She came up blank, her conscience clear. She was not a rule-breaker, unless forgetting last week's contribution to the tea and biscuits kitty counted... People said nothing got past him, but Rose wasn't buying into the omnipotent rubbish.

She shrugged off the panic that had grabbed her by the throat and told herself that the explanation would be something perfectly mundane, and she was pretty sure that Zac Adamos's interest in chocolate digestives was not extensive. Now, if she'd been a six-foot blonde with endless legs it might have been different, but she definitely wasn't...and even if she had been the sort of statuesque beauty he was often seen with, it was well known that he had never dated an employee.

Though she knew several that wouldn't have minded, excluding herself, of course. She was looking for something beyond superficial attractiveness and charisma so he would never get to know about her indifference... Her cushiony lips curved into a fleeting smile of self-mockery as she thought about a world where she would get a chance to say thanks but no thanks to Zac Adamos... *That* world didn't even exist in her dreams.

No, growing up watching her father use and then discard women meant the things that she was searching for in a man were safety and solidity. Of course, if he looked nice that wouldn't be a deal breaker!

Nice was not something anyone was ever likely to call her boss. He might be respected in the business world, but she suspected that respect was based on fear, which made her despise him even though her personal contact could hardly be rated as even negligible. She had once observed him striding past her down a corridor, and once standing in a lift looking impatient as he waited for the doors to close. On that occasion she had had the opportunity to study him without fear of being caught in the act because there was no harm in looking.

'I have d-done n-nothing,' she stammered out, thinking, beyond a bit of casual ogling.

The stutter managed to cancel out any defiant confidence, making her sound guilty or pathetic instead, probably both.

Her stammer was history but in moments of stress and heightened emotion it resurfaced. 'And I c-can't afford to lose this job.'

'There are other jobs.'

'You think I'm being sacked?'

'Of course not,' Jac tacked on hastily. 'I'm just saying sometimes a change is good, a new challenge…?'

'I like it here.' If it works why change it?

She loved what she did and, while every day was different because that was the nature of working with children, there was a comforting familiarity to it, something that her life as a child had lacked.

'So do I, but I've thought about it.'

Rose's eyes flew wide. 'You'd leave?'

The older woman's lips quirked at Rose's shocked response. 'I've been here seven years now and I feel in a bit of a rut. It was the extra half-hour commute that put me off.' She patted her stomach. 'I thought when the girls started secondary school, but with this one…who knows? But nothing is stopping you—you've got no one.' Realising what she'd said, she added hastily, 'Not that you couldn't have if you wanted.'

'I've no craving for excitement or a significant other,' Rose said, thinking of the *exciting* days of arriving home from school and finding it wasn't home any more and her things haphazardly dumped in her dad's car or, more often than not, left behind. And then there were the notes she found scribbled in her dad's bold hand telling her that he was spending the weekend in Paris or wherever had taken his fancy and to be a good girl and don't answer the door to anyone and there was a tenner for a takeaway.

There wasn't always a note.

On one no-note occasion the usual few days had stretched into ten. The memory could still shake loose the cold feeling of panic in the pit of her stomach when she began to wonder if this time he wasn't coming back, if she was alone now.

The effort of maintaining the pretence at school that everything was normal had made her feel physically ill. She'd tried to keep her head down and perfect the art of invisibility, a formula ruined after her dramatic faint in morning assembly, which might have been due to the stress or maybe the fact she'd been permanently hungry on a diet of tinned soup and baked beans.

Her dad had strolled back the next day as though he had just been to the corner shop.

'Hadn't time for a note, love. A free flight, private jet to Las Vegas, I wasn't going to say no to that, was I?'

That had been his breezy reaction to her tears of relief when he had reappeared after a ten-day absence.

He had handed her a diamond bracelet that was wildly inappropriate for a fourteen-year-old, then reclaimed it, much to her secret relief, on hearing the news that the headmistress wanted to see him the next day.

'Can't you put her off? I have sleep to catch up on. *You* breaking a rule? What have you been up to?'

'I forged your signature on my report card.'

'Oh, for heaven's sake. How hard is it to forge a signature?' he'd exclaimed, his generosity evaporating as he'd put the bracelet in his own pocket because she hadn't deserved it.

No, Rose had a very poor opinion of excitement. She was, as her dad often told her, *boring*. Frequently adding, *'I sometimes wonder if you're actually mine,'* presumably in case she hadn't got the message she was a massive disappointment to him.

'I'll miss you if you go.'

'In three years' time you probably won't be here yourself. You'll have moved on, found a gorgeous man, a beautiful thing like you...'

'I'm not looking.'

'I'd noticed,' the older woman said drily. 'It doesn't do to keep *the* man waiting, or so I've heard. Relax, I'm joking. It'll probably be an assistant or something.'

Rose's spirits lifted. Jac was right, anything to do with a lowly nursery nurse would be delegated. She didn't want to admit, even to herself, that the rush of relief she wouldn't see Zac Adamos was related to a conversation she had overheard the previous week as two women had blocked her access to a lift.

'I am quite literally shaking...my skin feels...'

Rose, wary of the flu bug going around, had taken a step backwards as the second woman had responded with a giggle.

'He's just so, so *sexy*…it's unbelievable. It hits you like a sonic boom…that mouth…mmm!'

'What wouldn't I give to work on the top floor and see him every day?'

'You'd never get any work done,' her friend had retorted as they'd wandered away.

Rose, who had identified the person with the sonic boom halfway through the conversation, now had access to the lift. She hesitated then headed for the healthy option, the stairs.

Not just for the exercise. Zac Adamos was not the healthy option. Compared to the Greek billionaire, her dad was in the minor leagues…actually probably no league at all. She'd read an article online that had called Zac Adamos a legend in his own lifetime, and if everything she'd read was half true he'd be the first to agree with this assessment. Humility and modesty were two words not associated with him.

Short of a push, nothing would have got Rose through the open door at the end of the boardroom had she not known the tall, supercilious blonde was watching. The woman had recoiled when she'd taken in the person waiting for her attention.

When it had come, the snooty smirk had been preceded by an icy, 'I think you might have the wrong floor.'

Rose, who wished she had got off on the wrong floor, had lifted her chin and given her name. She wasn't going to do meek for a fully paid-up member of the fashion police.

The woman's eyebrows had shot to her smooth hairline as she'd consulted her computer screen. '*You're* Miss Hill?'

She wouldn't give the sneering superior blonde the satisfaction of knowing that apprehension was making her knees knock.

Should I have knocked?

The thought came to her halfway through the door and caused her to stumble and lurch into the room.

Hands wide to steady herself, she managed not to fall flat on her face. The flick of the smile of relief faded before it formed as she looked across the room, a room that actually dwarfed the dimensions of the boardroom she had just walked through.

The impressive dimensions and the stunning glass wall made only a vague impression. It was the man who rose from his negligent pose behind a massive desk occupied by computer screens that dominated the space and her focus.

A big room but *not* a safe distance!

He looked impressive on a TV screen, in a Hollywood heart-throb kind of way. Rose had watched him out of idle curiosity as much as anything else—that and the fact such occasions were a rarity. He didn't court publicity, which made any interview he gave compulsive viewing—perhaps that was his intention, a variation on treat them mean, keep them keen.

From her armchair position she knew that he was possibly the most handsome man ever to draw breath.

She knew that he had a way of moving that was fascinating, all restrained power and elegance. She knew about the sculpted structure of a face that was arresting from any angle, all fascinating angles and intriguing planes, a masterful straight nose, carved cheekbones, his sensually sculpted wide mouth, his glowing golden-toned olive skin that matched the rich dark hair that sprang from his broad forehead and curled into his neck.

What she hadn't known was that his sloe-dark gaze framed by long ebony lashes and set below thick straight brows could paralyse a person's faculties.

She hadn't known that his sheer masculinity, the whipcord-lean male strength of his long, lean body not disguised by the perfect tailoring, could send a quiver through a person's body until it coalesced in a warm quiver in their pelvis…

No, Rose, not a person, you. Own it—your pelvis.

It took Rose a breath-suspended moment to recognise the disturbing sensation of unfurling desire sliding through her body.

Ashamed and shocked, she shook her head to free herself from the sensual fog and, realising that her mouth was open, closed it.

Wow, that was embarrassing, she thought as she rearranged her features into an expression of cool, polite interest. Boom! Sonic—definitely!

And she wasn't interested.

'You wanted to see me?' She tried to direct her

gaze to a point over his left shoulder but that hard dark stare had a mesmeric quality... No man should have eyelashes that long.

CHAPTER THREE

AFTER ARTHUR HAD apparently lost his magic touch, Zac had been forced to personally intervene and virtually beg the outgoing nanny, who was standing, bags packed, at the door, to stay until tonight. That had not sat well with him, plus he was irritated that the information Marco had sent over had been partial at best because he apparently didn't want to prejudice Zac's judgment. For Zac this translated as 'make my life more difficult'. And as for facts being prejudicial…?

He found it easy to shift his frustrations onto the woman who already had a black mark for tardiness.

Zac didn't appreciate being kept in the dark, and as for his impartiality… He let out a measured sigh. He could not blame Marco, who didn't know Zac's plan… The additional information would have been useful as he couldn't allow just anyone into his home with access to the baby.

Sure, her work record was clean but, and it was a big but—if he'd been brought up by his own father he had wondered what man he would be now—she *had* been raised by her father. Not that he could compare a minor league conman and chancer with a brutal, violent, drug-addled character who thought the practical solution to an unwanted pregnancy was to beat up his pregnant girlfriend.

He sighed. Earlier this had seemed a win-win situation but now…?

Then she fell into the room and he discovered that once you got past the trainers, jeans that clung to long legs, and a weird baggy thing with lurid handprints all over topped by a denim jacket that was several sizes too big for her petite frame, the woman standing there was identical to her elegant twin, who he already knew was an incredibly beautiful woman.

While he had been able to acknowledge the beauty of his friend's wife, he could enjoy her company while not being attracted to her. The beautiful glowing princess he had met was a work of art with a good sense of humour had been his objective assessment.

Given they were genuinely identical, he ought to be feeling the same way now. Instead there was no objectivity to the instant and powerful physical reaction he was experiencing to this terribly dressed copy with a cloud of untamed titian hair that floated around her vivid face,

Identical but not, he mused, searching her face for some defining feature, although there was none. Perhaps it was the depth of her wide-spaced eyes, a shadow that suggested mystery that drew him in, and the way she looked up at him through her lashes…

part of the indefinable additional factor that his body reacted to so spectacularly? Whatever it was, the indefinable *something* about her bypassed all logic circuits in his brain and pressed the primal button.

His shoulders lifted in a fractional shrug, a faint smile quivering along the firm sensual line of his mouth that contained self-mockery as he rose to his feet, gesturing with one long-fingered hand for her to take a seat. Sure, this was a complication, but one he was confident he could deal with.

Unlike some men he did not find the forbidden-fruit attraction an added turn-on, and he never had any problem walking away from such complications. There were plenty of women who were not already attached.

As his eyes drifted of their own accord to her truly sensational cushiony lips he found himself wondering if this woman was in a relationship, or if her attitude to sex was more *casual*, like his own.

There was something in her eyes, the suggestion of a vulnerability, that made him doubt it, though presumably Marco would know. If so, it was included in the information he had redacted so as not to bias Zac's judgment.

Rose was aware that Zac Adamos was a tall man with a lean, long-limbed body, an impressive physique that was frequently discussed in the many articles written about him. She'd always found it amusing that a piece on the financial markets had included the height—six feet four and a half—of the man whose opinion could influence these volatile monetary institutions—if he'd been a woman his age would have been added.

Only he wasn't!

As he unfurled himself from the chair, his every movement screaming graceful, restrained power, Rose felt her heart rate thicken to a dull thud, nerve endings across her skin tingled and the pull between her legs sent her into a shocked state of denial.

She hadn't taken a seat. She continued staring at him with an animal-in-the-headlights golden gaze. He found himself staring back, wondering as heat licked down his body how the pure amber of her eyes would look glazed with passion, half closed. And it took effort to get the question out of his head, not soon enough to spare him some discomfort—he was rock-hard...

Theos! Are you a man or a teenager?

Instead of walking towards her, he edged his behind onto the desk and, stretching his long legs out in front of him, waited—in part because he was aroused but mostly because people, in his experience, felt a need to fill a silence. Silence could access more information than a volley of questions.

This instance proved no exception. Words fell from her lips, lots of words but not necessarily in the right order. She had an attractive low, husky voice that had a soft, skin-tingling timbre.

'I...I'm sorry for w-wasting your time. I think

there's been a mistake. I think you probably want someone else…'

'No. I want you.' It was an indulgent play on words but he could not resist it. Not the time for games, his internal voice suggested, and, judging by the expression on her face, definitely not the sort of game she played.

Rose drew a deep breath and bit her lip, unable to hide her discomfort, but at least she didn't drop her gaze, comforting herself in the knowledge that he had no idea of the shameful direction of her thoughts after her wayward brain's wilful misreading of his innocent statement…

Could words from a mouth like his be innocent?

'So, tell me, do you enjoy your work?'

He'd asked her here to check if she liked her work…? Was this some sort of box-ticking HR exercise—they chose some random employee and asked them if they were happy?

'I l-love it.'

Her voice, even rushed, was pleasant to listen to, the huskiness emphasised by the stuttering snags that he found attractive.

'You love working with children all day?'

She nodded, wondering from his tone if maybe he didn't like children. It was certainly hard to imagine him with grubby finger-marks on his pristine pale grey suit or his tie askew…from chubby toddler hands anyhow, she mused, seeing long fingers and beautifully manicured red nails removing his clothes. It was an image that made it hard to focus on his response.

'So you have no ambitions to change your job?'

He saw alarm flare in her eyes and waited for her response, distracting himself by staring at her cushiony mouth, which was another thing he had not factored into this particular equation.

It would be a betrayal to follow up—a good enough reason to exert some self-control. Friendship was a more valuable and rarer commodity than lust, even a lust that was as visceral as this, he reminded himself as his eyes drifted back to her mouth. It was a temptation that his libido escaping its leash reacted to.

He had to rein it in.

Marco would never forgive him.

The reminder was a mental version of a cold shower, helpful but not a cure.

Forget the cure, all he needed was sleep. The reason for his lack of control afforded Zac some level of comfort, but sleep deprivation was not an excuse that Marco would accept. The Crown Prince's protective instincts for his wife would almost certainly extend to her twin.

'I have been reading your file.'

Rose's eyes widened. She had a file?

'It is impressive.' And very slim, though someone whose notes sounded pompous mentioned little ambition to progress and poor leadership qualities. 'Miss Hill, are you all right with me calling you Rose?'

It would seem she didn't rate a full smile, but

the lopsided half version was quite something even though the calculated charm did not warm his eyes. It clearly hadn't crossed his mind that she'd say no.

And of course she wouldn't even if she wanted to, and she did because she really *didn't* want to hear him say her name, roll it around his tongue in the way he had. She didn't want that to an extent that she recognised was totally disproportionate.

The question of *why* the sound of her name on his lips should make her skin prickle with antagonism was a question for a later date. It made as little sense as her embarrassingly visceral reaction to him. She was repelled by what he represented, a too good-looking man who possessed effortless charisma and no conscience, and, at the same time, attracted by the fact he looked like a fallen angel...if attraction was the right word for the itch under her skin.

The collision of opposites in her head was enough to give anyone a headache and she had one digging its claws into her temples at that moment.

What she needed was a couple of painkillers and a darkened room to fend off a migraine, the first in months and the last had been pretty torrid. She was too stressed to wrap up the truth as anxiety sparked defiance.

'It depends... If you're going to sack me, then no, you can't.'

He blinked and then laughed, the softening of his features as he gave vent to his amusement making him appear a lot younger. It didn't last, a moment later the hard calculating stare was back.

'Do you have a guilty conscience, Miss Hill?'

If only!

The shock of the maverick thought that popped unbidden into her head widened her eyes. But she couldn't ignore the pain stabbing at her temples, which was in danger of becoming as much of a worry as her dormant hormones springing into painful life. Perhaps the two were connected? Did physical primitive chemical responses give you a headache? Or maybe she was allergic to his overwhelming masculinity.

'I have no idea why I'm here.'

But I really wish I weren't.

She spoke so quietly that he strained to catch what she had said. 'Are you all right?'

It came less like concern and more like an impatient criticism, leaving Rose with the impression that it would be an inconvenience if she wasn't all right. It was an attitude she was familiar with; her dad had always acted as though on the rare occasions she had got ill she'd done so deliberately just to annoy him.

She lifted her chin, the irrational conviction that she would prefer to die than admit a weakness to this man rising to the surface. It would serve him right if she fainted away at his feet, though he would probably just step over her, and she had never fainted with migraine although she had thrown up. She pushed the alarming thought away.

'I'm fine.'

He shrugged and accepted her words at face value. It was possible she was always that pale or maybe she was a party animal and had a hangover from the previous night.

'I will get to the point. Firstly, I am not sacking you, secondly, I am offering you a job, though nothing of a permanent nature, more a…temporary placement.'

Her brow stayed furrowed and not just because of the throb in her temples. 'A what?'

'I have need of a nanny.'

'Aren't you a bit old?' She regretted the quip the moment it left her lips and his expression suggested he wasn't impressed. 'Sorry,' she murmured.

'I have become the guardian of a baby, a six-week-old boy… His parents are dead and the person employed to look after him is leaving.'

He watched the last remnant of the antagonism she was struggling to hide melt away. 'Oh, I am so very sorry.'

Her tender heart ached for the orphaned child. His expression did not invite sympathy but she felt it anyway, which a moment before she would have thought impossible. 'There are agencies…'

'I am aware,' he returned tersely, realising as he responded that the alternative plans he'd had in reserve to fulfil his promise to Marco should his first attempt not work would not be needed. Rose Hill had a weak spot, and he had found it: she was a bleeding heart. She was leaking empathy from every pore.

Zac felt no compunction about exploiting this weakness, and he doubted he would be the first to do so. It was not his business how many men had

found their way into her bed via a hard-luck story,
not that he was heading for her bed…or even his con-
veniently close desk, he reminded himself.

Marco would never forgive him.

'However, the fact that I am moving to Greece
complicates the situation.'

'Greece!' she exclaimed, unaware of the wistful
expression on her face as she immediately imagined
the romance of white sand, blue sea and bluer skies,
ancient history.

Zac could almost see her heart racing beneath
her denim jacket. Under the layers he imagined her
skin warm and smooth, only for a second but long
enough to make him impatient with his lack of control and the cause of it.

'Have you ever been there?'

'No, I haven't been anywhere… I mean, I've not
travelled much.' Actually, not at all, but she saw no
reason to invite another sardonic brow lift.

'My present flat is not a suitable environment for
a child.' That truth he had already recognised but
the solution had been something to be dealt with
down the line. *Would* Greece be a realistic suitable
solution? he wondered. This could actually be a test
run of the viability. He could stay in London during
the week and commute at the weekend. After all, a
young child wouldn't notice if he was there or not.

'So you are moving to Greece?' She glanced
around the office. She had no idea how that would
work, but his life had different rules from her own.
Even so she did admire him, despite her prejudices,

for being prepared to accept such a massive change to his life.

'It might not be a permanent solution but in the short term until the baby has…' he paused, trying to recall the phrase the nanny had used '…established a routine,' he offered glibly.

When lying it was always better to stick as close to the truth as possible and his solution to Marco's request had pushed his own thinking about the future along, and with those thoughts came nagging, actually *screaming* doubts.

Zac was not a man who lacked confidence or self-belief, and finding himself in a situation that he felt unqualified for on so many levels was disconcerting. Parenthood was something he had never envisaged and he felt uniquely ill equipped for the role.

Yet he had an excellent example. Kairos had been his age when he had taken on another man's son, and that man had been no friend. Had it come naturally to him or had he had to work at it? He dismissed the possibility before it had taken root in his head. Kairos had been a natural at parenting—he let his children make their own mistakes but had always been there to offer advice if they asked for it.

Zac made mistakes but he never asked for advice. Asking for help equated in Zac's head with admitting to a weakness. It was not something that the *tough one* did… Sometimes the roles assigned to children in families were hard to shrug off in adulthood.

In his case Zac hadn't tried—showing weakness

in the world in which he operated was not the road
to success.

'I need someone qualified to step in—'

'Why me?' she cut across him with the blunt question as she heard Jac groan in her head. She imagined
her friend's reaction to her hesitation.

*Don't ask why, just grab it with both hands!
Travel, get paid for it, what's not to like? Out of
your comfort zone? About time!*

'Not that I would be the right person.'

'That's an unusual interview technique you have
there.'

His drawl brought a flush to her cheeks but she
didn't drop her gaze. 'It's not an interview.'

One dark brow lifted. 'Pedantic but true,' he
conceded. 'But the situation does preclude a long
drawn-out process and, contractually, it would sim-
plify things. You already work for me. I don't need
references or security checks.'

'I'm sorry but—'

'You have no dependents…elderly parents…?'

'My father is alive, but he isn't…he doesn't need
me.' Until the next time he needs money or a bed
or… He'd never find her in Greece. Ashamed of the
thought, she added firmly, 'But I'm sorry, my life is
here. I'm not interested in going to Greece. It's out
of the question.'

He sighed. 'That is a pity—your choice, but, quite
honestly, probably the right one. He's not an easy
baby, he doesn't sleep… It's almost as if he knows
that he's alone.'

She felt an ache in her throat as she watched him lift a hand to shade his eyes. Just because he didn't show his emotions didn't mean he didn't have them, she thought, feeling a surge of empathic warmth.

Fighting the crazy impulse to lay a hand on his shoulder, she held her ground and cleared her throat. 'He's not alone, he has you,' she husked out firmly.

'I know nothing about... I'll learn.'

'Of course you w-will,' she agreed, thinking, What next? A herd of pigs flying overhead? I feel sorry for Zac Adamos.

Zac heard the emotional catch in her voice and thought, *Gotcha.*

His hand fell away, his long elegant brown fingers briefly catching and holding her attention. When her gaze lifted he appeared sombre but composed and thankfully unaware of the distracting tactile image that had floated into her head that involved his fingers against pale skin.

'Well, thank you for your...' He paused, dragged a hand through his dark hair and added as an almost embarrassed afterthought, 'Look, it probably won't make any difference to your decision, but because of the lack of notice and upheaval I am prepared to offer an exit bonus.'

The hook was in; all he had to do was reel her in.

'It's not the money—'

He mentioned a sum that made her jaw drop.

'That is a lot of money.' And after her dad's visit she didn't even have a *little* money.

'Not to me.'

It wasn't a boast, just a statement of fact.

He watched the emotions flicker across her face and concealed his sense of triumph. She had a soft heart, he could have worked the sympathy vote, but the money had swung it. Would this count against her in Marco's eyes? He didn't see why it should. Everyone had a price.

Rose took a deep breath. 'All right, I'll do it, but for half that amount.'

He blinked. 'Pardon me?'

'It's too much.'

He fought off a smile of disbelief—she had a price, but it was relatively low. The likelihood of Marco's sister-in-law being a gold-digger seemed fairly remote. 'As you wish.'

'Greece…?' she said in a wonder-packed voice. 'I'm going to Greece.'

Her travelling had always been done from the security of her armchair with a laptop propped on her knee while she planned trips she'd never be able to afford. And even if she had, she wasn't sure she was brave enough to venture to exotic places alone. She always thought about what would go wrong. It was a mindset from her childhood when the parent child roles had been reversed—her dad hadn't thought what might go wrong and someone had to, so she had become, as her father termed it, *the voice of doom.*

'You are helping me out of a difficult situation. I'm grateful.'

Is she for real? he asked himself, watching through half-lowered lids as her golden eyes misted.

Anyone who wore their emotions so close to the surface the way she did might just as well walk around with a sign pinned to their back saying, *Take advantage of me!*

Which was exactly what he was doing.

Though in a benign way, he reminded himself, pushing away the scratch of guilt, and instantly feeling irritated that he felt the rare need to justify his actions to himself.

She swallowed a lump in her throat. It was less what he said and more what he wasn't saying that made her tender heart squeeze.

'What is the baby's name?' she asked quietly.

'Declan.'

She nodded and he watched her soft, sensual mouth quiver. 'A lovely name.'

He nodded, lowering his lids to hide the gleam of triumph in his eyes. 'Your passport is up to date?'

'Pass…oh, yes, I think so.'

'Think or know?' he cut back.

'Know.' On the receiving end of his obsidian-dark stare, she struggled to know her name, and doubts flicked through her head. There was no hint of the emotional vulnerability that had swung her decision in his face now. 'So will you…?'

'Let you know the details, yes.'

She waited but that, it seemed, was all she was getting. He seemed to have tuned her out as he retreated to the other side of the big desk, tapping something into his phone and focused on the screen.

Wondering what she had committed herself to, Rose picked up the bag that she had no memory of dropping at her feet. She turned and glanced over her shoulder, awkwardly and belatedly aware of the questions she should have asked, but it would seem that the moment to ask them had passed. He was speaking in a language that was Greek to her, and might actually have been.

In a daze she walked out of the room, her trainers squeaking on the polished wood floor of the echoey boardroom, the questions that she'd failed to ask a few moments ago buzzing in her head like a swarm of wasps.

She was already having buyer's remorse or second thoughts. She'd taken a leap in the dark and it did not feel liberating, it felt awful. It swallowed up the excitement of the chance to travel, leaving only anxiety.

Why had she said yes? OK, the money *had* been a practical factor, but turning her back on someone's need, their plea for help, even if that someone was Zac Adamos, was something her soft heart simply wouldn't allow her to do.

She tried to imagine anyone saying no to Zac Adamos and felt slightly less feeble. It had probably never happened, but she'd love to witness it when it did. She could empathise with his situation but that didn't mean that she thought he was any less of an arrogant and up-himself narcissist.

The woman with the snooty attitude and the

blonde hair pretended not to see her as she walked past so Rose returned the compliment and promptly felt silly and petty, but she didn't feel up to taking the high ground.

The first loo she saw she ducked inside, glad there were no executive types to stare at her. She went over to the vanity basins, and after a face-to-face confrontation with her pale-faced, wild-haired self in the mirror she made sure not to repeat the experience as she balanced her bag on the edge of the washbasin and rummaged through the contents, which was always an adventure in itself. She gave a small grunt of triumph as she found a strip of bog-standard painkillers in one of the zipped compartments, not her prescription meds for migraine but hopefully it would fend off an attack, or at least slow down the inevitable.

Rose swallowed them without water, contemplating as she choked on them a little the result if she walked back into Zac Adamos's office and told him she'd changed her mind… Had she changed her mind?

Rose sighed. She was not a 'jump in without thinking through the consequences' sort of person. It was just so unlike her to make a decision without reading the small print.

'It's only a few weeks,' she told her reflection, then frowned as she realised she didn't know how many. 'You might enjoy it.'

She sighed and thought, And now I'm talking to myself! Not a good start. The mockery faded from her eyes as she thought of the start in life the baby had. She struggled to see Zac Adamos as a hands-on parent. The poor little scrap would probably go straight from nannies to boarding school.

Catching herself in the act of inventing a scenario that cast the tall Greek in a poor light just because she didn't like the man, Rose felt a stab of unease. She didn't normally think the worst of people, and this Greece project showed he was making an effort. It must be hard. He'd tragically lost friends and found himself with a ready-made family, and being a single parent was not easy, even for someone with limitless funds, a category her boss fell into. But, obscenely rich or not, you couldn't buy the support that came from having a partner to share parental responsibilities.

Or maybe you could? Rose was sure that any number of those leggy beauties he squired—or, more accurately, had sex with—would be happy to co-parent if it involved having a big rock on her finger.

Knowing she was being uncharitable but unable to stop the catty thoughts, Rose exited the loo, passing a couple of elegant women as she did so. They stared but she barely noticed. Her tangled thoughts left no space in her head for anything else.

CHAPTER FOUR

THE ELUSIVE SCENT—something flowery but not sweet—lingered in the office after she had left. The attraction was there, so he would acknowledge it.

As if he had much option, considering he was still semi aroused!

Acknowledge and move on, even without Marco's red line. Zac would never act upon it. The charming, serene princess's twin was the sort of woman he avoided, the sort of woman who did not consider sex a physical transaction.

He was pretty sure the redhead was into deep and meaningful. It was written all over her. In short she was *exactly* the sort of woman his mother hoped he would meet.

Having sorted out where she fitted in the scheme of things, he felt more comfortable, his boundaries back in place. Obviously he would need to be in her company but only to observe…that was after all what Marco wanted. *No touching, Zac.*

Thinking of his friend, he contacted Marco to give him a progress report.

'So she'll be living under your roof? That's ideal.'

To Zac it was not. To have a woman who was the mirror image of one whose identical lips he had never fantasised about tasting, crushing, but was out of bounds was not at all ideal in his book. Painful, yes.

'First impressions, Marco...' The impression he intended to pass on to his friend would obviously have some exclusions. Marco might not be happy if Zac included the fact that the woman he was assessing was a living, breathing threat to any man's sexual control. 'For what it's worth I don't think you have anything to worry about.'

'You don't think there's any danger to Kate? Her father came across as very plausible...'

Danger. The only person that he could see Miss Rose Hill being a danger to, other than his libido, was herself. But what did he know? Maybe it was an act, maybe she had learnt the skill of deception from her father—the negotiating her bonus down might just be a clever ruse... He had been the target of women before, perhaps it was all an act to get his attention...?

On the other hand, she might be determined *not* to be her father. Or had she inherited the flaws of her parent?

Was the fear always there in the back of her mind that she might have inherited the genetic fingerprint of her father? *No, Zac, that's you*, mocked the voice in his head.

'First impressions, Marco, I can't see inside her

head, but she doesn't come across as a con artist, but then,' he conceded, 'I suppose really good ones don't.'

'Sorry if I sound—'

'Paranoid? No offence. I understand.' Except of course he didn't. He had never felt protective in that way about any woman in his life aside from his mother, not even come close, but then all the women that drifted in and out of his life could look after themselves.

Marco's tired-sounding laugh echoed down the line. 'None taken and I *am* very grateful, I don't want to risk—'

'How is Kate?'

The rest of their conversation, which Zac brought to a close by inventing an urgent appointment, concerned the health of Marco's wife and her seeming perfection, which made Zac imagine her twin wearing the sort of priceless bling around her neck that the princess did. Rose wasn't wearing anything else except her glorious hair and the sultry smile of invitation he had not seen but had imagined curving her plump lips.

As he stood gazing out at the City panorama, the imaginary image in his head lingered.

It was totally inexplicable, not a little insane and very primal the way that woman had burrowed her way under his skin. Perhaps this was a version of love at first sight for a man who didn't fall in love—*lust* at first sight, which luckily for him didn't have the same staying power.

He remembered chastely kissing Kate Zanetti on her fragrant cheek and feeling zero desire to lay her across his desk, which was probably just as well because he was sure that if Marco had issues with Zac lusting after his sister-in-law, his wife would be a pistols-at-dawn scenario.

He valued his friendship with Marco, and it wasn't as if his friend were asking for a kidney. A few weeks of keeping his libido on a leash and his objectivity front and centre to ease Marco's fears was not a big ask. He was walking around the desk when he saw the glint of metal, a bunch of keys lying on the wooden floor, and he bent down to retrieve the object. Not his keys. Only one person in his office today would have a key ring that was attached to a knitted stuffed animal—it could have been a pig, or it might have been a horse...?

He reached out to press the button on the intercom and stopped as an image appeared of Rose Hill standing on her doorstep rummaging through her bag, and realising she'd lost her keys. It was easy to imagine the panic in her spectacular eyes. It was even easier to imagine passion, the slow burn that sparked into a full-blown conflagration. He thought about her slim, expressive hands touching... He was so absorbed by the image in his head that for a split second he forgot his pledge not to want her, but was saved from this self-indulgent torture by the sound of his PA's voice. He lifted his finger off the button he had not been aware of pressing and responded.

'No, it's fine. I'm...actually I'm leaving early.' As

he made his way through the building he contacted Arthur and explained the bare bones of the situation and what arrangements he needed putting into place.

Zac could not recall entering the crèche in this or any other of the Adamos buildings. They came under the umbrella of the Adamos Trust, one of the charitable trust's less challenging projects and one he took little personal interest in. Closer to home was the adult literacy programme—one of his half-sisters was dyslexic.

The brightly painted walls and cheerful artwork on them certainly set it apart from the rest of the minimalist pale building. Long-term exposure would have given him a headache. He had just passed a particularly vibrant collage, obviously produced in-house by childish hands, when he came to a door that said *'Office'*. The upper panel was glass, the bottom urged the reader in big letters to *'Come right in'*.

One dark brow lifted as Zac read the instructions, which in his view constituted taking informality several steps too far. Was the half-open door encouragement to barge in unannounced?

Zac was about to test out the theory when the sound of a voice within made him pause.

'So? What happened?'

'I'm sorry to leave you short-handed but—'

'He sacked you!' Jac went pink. 'Why, that…piece of slime. No, I'm not standing for this. I'm going right up there to give him a piece of my mind!'

Rose was touched by this passionate, if slightly

impractical, declaration of war on her behalf. 'Calm down.' She laughed, giving the older woman an affectionate hug as much as her bump allowed. 'He didn't sack me, he offered me a sort of temporary placement.'

'Oh, don't give me a scare like that...' Jac huffed out in relief, then as she pushed her owl-like glasses up her nose her brow furrowed. 'A placement?'

As Rose explained the situation, Jac's eyes went wider and wider behind the lenses of her specs. 'So you're going to Greece to look after this orphaned baby? That's so sad, not for you though, wow!' Her voice carried an even higher note of incredulity as she added, 'So now Zac Adamos is a *dad*? How is he dealing with it? Or need I ask? This is Mr Ice In His Veins.'

'Jac, that's not fair!' Rose protested, finding herself unable to appreciate the other woman's sense of humour. 'Just because someone doesn't show his feelings it doesn't mean he doesn't have any.'

'Oh, my God, Rose, why do you always think the best of people?'

'I don't...well, I know I do, but this is different. To be honest I'm really wary of working for him.'

'I can think of several people in the building who would feel differently,' the older woman suggested with a wry smile. 'So for how long are we going to be without you?'

'Actually, I'm not sure.' It would have been practical to ask but it didn't really matter. She had no ties except a father who only appeared when he wanted something.

She was a free agent, she told herself, ignoring the little ache that came with the thought. 'Until the nanny returns, I suppose.'

'But Greece and Zac Adamos...' The older woman rolled her eyes. 'If I was a few years younger...and maybe a couple of stone lighter, what wouldn't I give?'

Rose flushed, struggling to respond in the same jocular style. Her sense of humour on the subject was running low, and her laugh missed spontaneous and hit forced dead centre.

'You're welcome to him,' Zac heard her declare as he watched the speaker's mirror image shift her bag from one shoulder to the other.

'He is the last man in the world I'd be interested in!' she exclaimed.

Protesting just a little bit too much here, Rose. Anyone would think you're in denial.

Her chin lifted in response to the mocking voice in her head, then lowered from its jutting angle a moment later. She didn't *want* to find him attractive and it was true alpha males, which he undoubtedly was, did not appeal to her, at least in theory.

But she couldn't deny that walking into that office and meeting his eyes had caused her to experience the sort of skin-peeling sexual awareness she had only previously read about...and not really believed.

The worrying thing was that part of her had liked

the rush of skin-tingling excitement, it had made her feel alive, but another part of her had been scared.

But then aren't you always scared, Rose?

'Don't look so worried, Jac. I doubt he even noticed I'm female.' She remembered a glitter in his dark eyes before they were shielded by his lashes and wondered…

'That's the sweet thing about you, Rose.'

Rose's smile became fixed. To her way of thinking, when people said *'sweet'* they meant *'boring'.*

'You have no idea that you're gorgeous.'

Rose's fleeting irritation became embarrassment. 'I'm excited—it's a fantastic opportunity,' she said, steering the conversation into less personal channels.

'Just be careful.'

'Careful?'

'Our boss, he's the big fish, a classic Great White, all teeth and no conscience. He can be charming, but—'

'I didn't rate his charm,' Rose cut in, her nose wrinkling as she added, 'and I may be *sweet*—' her lips moved in a moue of distaste '—but I'm not dim. I know what he is…but then who wouldn't be a bit up themselves if they looked in the mirror every day and saw that face?' An image of the fascinating angles and strong planes floated through her mind. What would it feel— She cancelled the rogue line of thought before it progressed into dangerous territory. 'But honestly, Jac, if I *was* looking, which I'm not,' she tacked on hastily.

'Why the hell not? Is it that ratbag Sutton? Oh, for goodness' sake, Rose, don't let him put you off men.'

'No, of course not.' The Andy Sutton incident was not one of the finer moments in life, but in the scheme of things it hadn't been a big enough deal to *traumatise* her. She had even managed to laugh about it with Jac the Monday after the dinner party from hell. 'He blanked me the other day, you know.'

'Rat…slime ball.'

Rose laughed. 'I opened my mouth to say hello and he walked straight past as if I wasn't there.'

'What a total…' Jac growled.

'Well, I did embarrass him—his face when he saw I was wearing jeans and a tee shirt! They were my *best* jeans, and the tee shirt did have sequins.' She gave a small gurgle of laughter, though it hadn't seemed funny at the time. 'A casual dinner, he said.' Which turned out to mean one step down from black tie—the women had all been done up to the nines in designer dresses.

'He let you make your own way home in that rain.'

'I'm a big girl, Jac, and honest it's not because of him I'm not looking. If there is someone out there for me, I'll meet him and if not?' Her slender shoulders lifted, causing the bag slung across one shoulder to slip down her arm.

'Oh, my God, you're a romantic!' Jac despaired. 'Prince Charming doesn't come knocking on your door, you have to put yourself out there. All right,' she added, folding her arms across her generous breasts. 'So what would you be looking for, should you be looking.'

'Well, not a pretty face...'

Or even a beautiful one.

She blinked. The face that floated into her head was all angles, carved planes and intriguing hollows, and the effort it took to banish it made her scowl, her annoyance aimed at herself for allowing him space in her mind for free.

'And,' she continued, retrieving her thread, 'I'd like someone who can laugh at themselves.' She arched a satiric brow and heaved her bag more firmly on her shoulder. 'Can you see the Gorgeous Great White laughing at himself? Yeah, GGW. I like it.'

Catching sight of herself in the mirror, she groaned and lifted a hand to her fiery head. 'Why didn't you tell me to run a comb through my hair before I went up—' She stopped dead, her heart throwing off an extra thud before it promptly sank into the region of her trainers—hers wasn't the only face she saw reflected there.

Her life didn't flash before her eyes but every word of the exchange did.

'I would have knocked but the instruction seemed quite clear,' the GGW said, displaying his white even teeth.

The older woman leapt as if shot. Rose flinched. The guilty looks they exchanged gave him a certain satisfaction. It was not an ego-enhancing experience to hear yourself called *a pretty face who was a bit up himself.* Or that he was the *last* man Rose would be looking for. Luckily Zac's ego was pretty robust, although had the situation been different he might have enjoyed making Rose Hill eat her words.

His smile was, Rose decided, cruel. She couldn't understand why women went for bad boys. Not that he was a boy, he was all man… While she waited for the floor to open up at her feet the word *dangerous* floated through her head.

When the floor didn't open she fought the childish urge to close her eyes and become invisible—it had worked when she was five. Jac was no help. She appeared to have been struck dumb by shock. It made Rose feel slightly better to see she wasn't the only one who became a basket around this man.

Rose took a deep breath and did the only thing possible in the circumstances—she acted as if he hadn't heard a word they'd said. There was an outside possibility he hadn't, but if he had then that was his fault for *lurking*.

'I was just explaining to Jac about my temporary placement.' She glanced at Jac and hesitated. Despite Jac's admittedly cautious enthusiasm, she was probably thinking of the staffing headache that Rose's absence would cause when she went swanning off to Greece.

Her eyes narrowed and her chin firmed. 'I told her that you would be supplying a temp to fill in.'

Her steady golden stare challenged him to deny it. The sheer novelty of anyone attempting to manipulate him drew a grudging admiration and a grin from Zac. She had guts, he'd give her that.

'I will of course arrange a replacement, though I'm sure that our Miss Hill is irreplaceable.'

Unlike Rose, Jac didn't hear the sarcasm, but she had recovered her power of speech, and looked relieved and enthusiastic as she almost fell over herself in her eagerness to agree and paint Rose as a cross between Superwoman and a saint.

In the periphery of his vision Zac was amused to see Rose squirming with embarrassment at having her praises sung so loudly. It would seem this twin was not into self-promotion. Not knowing Kate well enough, he didn't know if this was a shared characteristic. The whole twin thing was fascinating—if twins were raised apart, did they turn out the same?

Ironic really that, from what Marco had revealed, the adopted twin had drawn the lucky straw on the parenting front, a caring family who were close and supportive, whereas this twin was raised by her biological father who could hardly be considered supportive, but Zac supposed she didn't know any different.

Rose forced a smile that left her eyes suspicious and wary. Jac didn't need to advise caution with this man, she had a brain, though admittedly not one that worked too well when she shared an enclosed space with him. His sheer overpowering physicality was rapidly undoing all the good work of the painkillers.

She took some comfort from the fact that his Greek home was not going to be a shoebox size... She was going to find out first-hand how the other half lived and she was curious, but not envious. She had lived in some pretty plush places over the years, depending on her dad's fortunes, and some pretty basic places too. Given the option she would have taken plush, but it didn't always equate with happiness.

One of the worst times she remembered growing up was when they were living in a lovely house in an upmarket area. Her dad had taken off to Paris and the *colleague* who had come looking for her absent parent had called her a pretty little thing in a really creepy, sinister way. She'd not dared turn on a light every night that week because she'd seen him hanging around outside—she had hated that house.

'I was just on my way home, Mr Adamos…?' Hands stretched palm upwards in a mystified gesture, she arched a questioning brow, though she was less interested in why he was here than him leaving— fingers crossed he would take the hint.

'Of course.' Before Rose could begin to guess his intention, he reached out casually and caught her right hand, his long brown fingers curling around her wrist. The brush of his thumb against her palm sent a zigzag of sensation along her nerve endings and she forgot how to breathe.

It was a weirdly out-of-body moment as Rose watched, as though it were happening to someone else, as he placed a bunch of keys in her palm and closed her fingers over them.

'I think you'll need these.'

The contact lasted only seconds but the effect on Rose was electric. She blinked and opened her hand, knowing that she was staring at the keys like an idiot but it was better than the option of looking up at him. That was something she was delaying until her nervous system had re-established some protective boundaries.

'Oh, I didn't know that I'd…thank you.' Until she opened her mouth she wasn't sure she would sound totally sane, because what else could you call her reaction to the fleeting contact if not insane? Relieved by her steady delivery, she addressed the comment to a point over his left shoulder while convincing herself that the skin-peeling tingle was just a symptom of stress, like a headache without the pain—she already had the headache.

'Not at all.'

Rose felt some of the tension leave her shoulders when he left the room with a clipped nod of his dark head.

'Oh, my goodness. You know, Rose, he's not really so bad, is he?'

His fiercest critic was won over by one smile. Rose rolled her eyes in despair. 'I thought he was a merciless GGW?' she observed drily.

CHAPTER FIVE

'Ah, Miss Hill. You are going home?'

Kill me now, Rose thought, closing her eyes and fixing an interested smile on her lips before she turned to face the tall figure who had materialised in the doorway. 'Yes…?' she said warily. He was half in and half out of the room but the disturbing skin tingling was sadly not halved.

She nodded, thinking he was not a shark and not white, he was more an olive gold, more a sleek, dangerous, unpredictable panther.

'Excellent,' he said briskly, turning his wrist to consult his wafer-thin expensive watch with narrowed eyes. She got a flash of lightly hair-roughened sinewy forearm as he appeared to make some silent calculation before fixing her with his deeply unnerving dark stare. 'I'm heading out myself, so as we're on the clock it will be simpler if I take you home and wait while you pack.'

It wasn't even couched as a suggestion! This man was utterly unbelievable.

And I am pathetic, she told herself as she *just*

stopped herself nodding in agreement. The man spoke and people jumped. You could sort of see why, she conceded, studying his face. It was no hardship, but she wasn't going to be one of that number.

He took a commanding personality to the next level. It was easy to see why people didn't question, they just went along without argument.

As he began to turn, clearly expecting her to follow, Rose, who was rarely the voice of dissent and hated confrontation, experienced an uncharacteristic surge of defiance, and along with it came a rush of resentment she hadn't even known she was nursing until it bubbled up like water under pressure to the surface.

She'd spent her life *following*, her opinion never even considered by her dad, and now she was always the one who said she didn't mind what pizza topping, what film… She told herself it didn't matter, they were inconsequential things, but it did matter.

There had to come a time to stop following and stand your ground.

You really choose your moments, Rose. She ignored the ironic voice in her head, her soft jawline firming as she pushed her hands deep in the pockets of her oversized jacket and, taking a deep breath, she dug her metaphorical heels in. Her teeth clenched. It had clearly never crossed his mind that she would not simply jump when he said jump—no please involved—or at least trot a few respectful feet behind him.

'Wait?'

He paused, turned and stepped back; sleek, exclusive and tall, he immediately dominated the room with his presence and his restless energy. Rose watched a flicker of impatience flash across his lean features but clung stubbornly to her calm defiance... Well, maybe not calm, she conceded as her heart flung itself against her ribcage. Despite her heart's contortions she felt strangely excited to be stepping outside her compliant role—*about time*, some, including Rose herself, might have said. His off-the-scale arrogance was the catalyst she had needed for this rebellion and how ironic was that!

'For you to pack,' he explained, glancing at his watch. 'You can meet the nanny. It will leave time for a handover this evening—she has agreed to stay that long.' Though it had taken the inducement of a chauffeur-driven limo to the airport and a first-class ticket to get this concession. 'Then we can leave in the morning. Arthur will go ahead.'

Her eyes had opened to their fullest extent by the time he had completed outlining this itinerary. She didn't know who Arthur was and didn't really care. It was less the arrangements and more the timescale that shocked her.

'*Tomorrow? Now?* B-but I assumed that this would be happening...' She made a fluttering gesture with her hands to indicate some vague point in the future, or at least next week.

One thick dark brow slanted. 'Is that a problem?'

'N-no.' She stopped—what was she saying? 'Actually yes, this is...too fast for me...it's happening very…very…' Hard to describe a sensation that felt like sand slipping through her fingers. She bit her lip and achieved something approaching calm as she said, 'I couldn't possibly be ready that soon.'

'We have already established you have no dependent relative. Is it a boyfriend who can't bear to let you go?' His expression made this possibility seem insultingly unlikely. 'A cat…?'

Oh, my, he had really pushed it too far. Her eyes narrowed into slits. 'I like cats but no, it isn't, and actually my personal life is none of your business.'

She fought off a laugh. He could not have looked more startled if a stray cat had turned around and told him to push off. Her amusement fizzled out fast, because the personal life she was guarding was pretty much a blank sheet, but that was a depressing thought for another time.

'Look, I appreciate that this is sudden,' he admitted, looking as if the concession hurt.

Big of you, she thought, panic colliding with resentment in her head, which ached with the sheer volume of emotions swirling inside… Hard to remember that when she had woken just this morning the only problem on her horizon had been that she'd mistakenly bought decaf coffee and that her overdraft would be nudging towards the danger red zone once she'd paid her electric bill. The bonus he'd offered, even halved, would solve all her problems.

'But the situation is urgent,' he said sombrely.

The reminder made the truculent heat fade from Rose's eyes and she felt ashamed for forgetting the reason for her trip to Greece. This was about an orphan baby, not her being forced to be decisive for once in her life.

Her internal struggle was written on her face, and she didn't have a clue she was being manipulated without any effort, which strangely left an unpleasant aftertaste in Zac's mouth. The faint scratch of guilt he felt was irrational. He hadn't lied, though in reality his situation would have warranted the odd white lie. If Rose backed out at this stage the childcare issue would be problematic. He ought to have made alternative childcare arrangements, but he rarely factored in failure, and he hadn't failed, he'd just pressed the button marked empathy plus a cash incentive—it always helped—and the rest had followed on as night followed day.

'I need time to think…'

Considering his promise to Marco, the last thing that Zac wanted was her thinking. He was impatient to fulfil his promise and get on with his life—his new life with the new responsibilities.

He had many responsibilities, the livelihoods, the future prosperity of many people rested on the decisions he made and he had never lost a night's sleep over the pressure, had never doubted his ability to come through, but this was different.

To keep a new life safe, to mould and guide it, Kairos made it look easy, but he was not his stepfather.

He was not his father either, his father who had not taken to the concept of parenthood. On discovering his very much younger girlfriend was carrying his child, giving her money for an abortion had been the sum of his paternal involvement, or *almost*. Because when he'd discovered the money intended for her abortion had been hidden away, he had tried to cause the same effect with his fists and feet.

His mother was a survivor and, despite what had happened to her when she was a teenager, an optimist.

'About what do you need to think?'

For the first time she was conscious of an accented undertone in his deep vibrant voice.

Did he make love in Greek?

The question came from nowhere and she felt her cheeks heat.

She could feel the impatience rolling off him in waves, but it wasn't a need to placate him that made her blurt out, 'Fine!' She wanted to prove to herself that she *could* step out of her comfort zone—if not now, when?

He accepted her compliance, deciding not to notice the reluctance involved, with a sharp tip of his dark head. He took a moment to say goodbye to Jac and stepped to one side for Rose to precede him through the door while she hugged her friend and said she'd see her very soon.

The touch of courtesy vanished as they stepped into the corridor—his long loping stride took no account of the difference in their inside leg measurements. Rose had to trot intermittently to keep up with him as they left the crèche and stepped into a lift that went down into the underground car park, entering an area that was reserved for people who drove shiny upper-end cars.

The one whose lights flashed as they approached was the higher end of upper, a low-slung thing as sleek as its owner. He opened the passenger door and left her to it as he walked around to the driver's side. As he did so her head turned when the corner of her eye caught two men standing by a car. One she recognised as the accountant—*Call me Andy*—who had ghosted her the previous week after the disastrous date.

As if in slow motion she saw his head turn her way. It was a reflex, no thought involved at all, when she ducked down into a crouching position behind the car.

The thinking started once she was there.

'Should I ask?'

Rose looked at the shiny handmade shoes just in front of her and thought, *Oh, someone kill me now, put me out of my misery!*

'Shall I join you?'

Oh, Rose *hated* him in that moment, hated him for having a front-row seat to her humiliation, and enjoying it.

'I take it that is the *slime ball*…?'

Things got worse—she could no longer pretend he hadn't heard every word.

'He's coming across,' Zac observed conversationally.

'Oh, God!'

'What's the problem? No possibility of misconstruing the situation, is there, you on your knees at my feet…?'

Rose, her cheeks burning bright, shot to her feet so quickly that she would have overbalanced if his hands had not cupped supportively around her elbows. There was barely a whisper of space between them and, looking at his chest, she stepped hastily back, or tried to as the grip on her elbows didn't loosen.

Rose's head tilted back to meet his dark stare. It was a dizzying experience…the lights dancing in his dark eyes had a hypnotic effect.

'Thanks, I'll take it from here.' She had to face the cringe situation. Who knew? Maybe she could extract a scrap of dignity out of it.

Not likely but possible. She had never told Jac that after the dinner party, previous to ghosting her, Andy had cornered her and suggested a threesome with one of the other dinner-party guests. A man who he declared was out of her league, who had liked her *style*…acting as if it were a compliment, not an insult! She had wanted so badly to slap his slimy smug face. Instead her stuttered response had drawn a mocking laugh from him and a *forget it* thrown over his shoulder.

'No, I don't think so. I have this one. You want to see him kick himself for not realising what he had? You want him to feel small and insignificant?'

Actually, now that he said it, that was exactly what she wanted, but it wasn't going to happen. 'Oh, God!'

Her sense of impending doom increased as she heard her name being called.

'I already knew what he did. I just didn't know until I overheard your conversation that the woman they were talking about was you.'

She looked at him in horror. Greece was not far enough, she would have to move to Alaska to escape the gossip!

'So that's a yes?'

'No, it's…' She sighed and nodded, humouring him.

'Let's do it, then.'

'What?' Rose's eyes widened as one of his big hands slid to her waist, the other curved around her face, tipping it up to him. He scanned the oval of her face for a moment, his restive glance finally landing on her lips and staying there.

Rose watched him, her vision blurring as his head bent until his mouth was a whisper away from hers… Her eyelids felt weighed down, so heavy she couldn't keep her eyes more than half open as she looked up at him. Her breath held inside her chest, her heart was hammering, pounding in her ears.

Zac released her waist, his expression intent as he stroked the cushiony softness of her full lower lip with the pad of one thumb, before bending his head and tugging the same spot with his teeth, the whisper touch, the sensual slide of his firm lips across the pouting curve sending a deep trembling quiver through her body.

She leaned into the pressure as the kiss deepened

and grabbed hold of his jacket to strain upwards, her senses absorbing the warmth and the hardness of his body. Flames burnt away rational thought, silencing the *This is a bad idea* as it was washed away by a dark sense of excitement exploding in her brain as she kissed him back.

Then it was over. He unwound her arms, which had crept up around his neck, and nodded over her shoulder.

Rose fell back on her heels, colour draining from her face and a moment later rising back until her cheeks burned. Mortified because she was shaking, the pulse between her legs still throbbing, her breasts tingling where they had been pressed into his chest, she resisted the impulse to touch her tingling lips. Echoes of the shocking intimacy of the moment were reverberating around her skull.

To add another layer of mortification, Zac, who was adjusting his shirt cuff, looked utterly cool.

'W-why…?' Her stuttered monosyllabic response covered most of the questions swirling around in her head.

Why had he kissed her, why had she kissed him back, why had she liked it…? Some of the answers were obvious even in her shocked state—she was no expert, but it seemed safe to assume, with her lips still tingling, that he was a good kisser.

Zac really found that stutter attractive, and with lips pumped up from the kiss, her eyes sparking, she looked— It did not matter what she looked like, he reminded himself. This was Marco's sister-in-law and as such off limits.

He had seen an opportunity and…en route to a smooth rationalisation of his actions his thoughts hit a truth roadblock. What he had seen was her mouth, the humiliation she had been trying to shrug off in her eyes, and the guy who had put it there.

He had wanted to flatten the guy right there and then. That not being an option in a civilised world, sadly, he had gone for the next best thing…give the loser a taste of his own medicine.

Zac, who considered himself a pretty good judge of character, had summed up the guy in one glance as a pretentious idiot with an inflated sense of his own importance. You could tell a lot from a glance, and when you'd heard his victim laugh about the humiliating experience—it had given meaning to the phrase *putting a brave face on it*.

And, less nobly, because he'd recognised a chance to satisfy his curiosity. Was he right to suspect there was a sizzling sensuality waiting to be coaxed into life? Turned out there was not much coaxing required.

And now he knew, which was a punishment in itself because the kiss was it. It was not going anywhere, he wouldn't allow it to. He'd lost one friend and he wasn't going to lose another. Marco would not approve of anything less than a saint for his sister-in-law and Zac was not a saint.

'I think that…what's his name…your boyfriend

is realising what he has missed, which is what you wanted…no?'

Zac, on the other hand, was realising what he could not have. He continued to feel the knowledge like a nerve exposed to cold air, and he only had himself to blame. Taking responsibility didn't cool the heat inside that had nowhere to go, or answer the one question in this self-confessional mode he was dodging, namely the strength of his reaction to the sight of the man who had humiliated Rose.

'He works for you and he's not my boyfriend.' She'd been wondering how much he'd overheard and now she knew—everything!

'He will tell everyone that he saw…' Her eyes slid from his. 'And by this time tomorrow just about everyone will know. They will think…' She looked at him, suspicion beginning to dawn in her bright eyes. 'That's what you wanted, isn't it?' The *why* remained.

He gave a magnificently unconcerned shrug. 'You are making a big thing of one little kiss,' he complained, unwilling to admit that he had broken one of his own cardinal rules. Hard to take the high ground when he had indulged in the sort of behaviour he would have condemned in anyone else—workplace liaisons never ended well.

Despite multiple examples that disproved the rule, Zac clung to this belief.

'Believe me, I know, by the time you get back to work this will be yesterday's news. For the life of me,' he added in a disgruntled tone, 'I have no idea why you're so bothered about what this guy thinks, unless you were hoping to take up where you left off?'

Rose drew in a wrathful indignant breath. 'I'm not that desperate!'

'I'm glad you know your own worth.'

She looked up at him expecting to see something smug or sarcastic in his face but there wasn't. He looked...*intense*...?

'And now,' he continued, 'your accountant knows that too. The punishment fits the crime, he's humiliated.' He watched her face. 'Because on the dating food chain I come a little higher than an accountant, shallow but true,' he added before she could respond. 'You can thank me another time.' He followed up the outrageous suggestion with a throaty laugh when she hid a smile behind her hand. 'Good to know that you're not all saint. Revenge can taste very sweet, can't it?'

So did he, she thought, the taste of him still in her mouth. He'd kissed her to teach Andy a lesson, but she'd learnt one too, an important one for her self-preservation, namely she was not at all indifferent to Zac Adamos and to kiss him for real would be very dangerous.

'Shall I sack him?'

She blinked at the casual offer.

'What?'

'Sack him.'

'You can't do that.'

'I think you'll find that I can... Oh, you mean the

legality? Don't worry, I'm sure he has crossed a line at some point…most people have.'

'Not me!' she snapped back huffily. 'You shouldn't judge people by your own standards.' Her eyes widened on his face in horror. 'I said that out loud, didn't I?'

'You did, but relax, and for the record I do not judge people by my own standards…most people have scruples.' He allowed his cynical gaze to move across her shocked and disapproving face. 'It gives me an advantage.'

Rose, her full lips still pursed in disapproval, had arranged herself in the cushioned leather luxury of a low-slung seat with a lot more leg room than she needed when Zac slid sinuously in.

He turned and looked at her, after a long silence finally voicing the question. 'Where do you live?'

'Oh, sorry!' She told him, expecting him to ask directions—the unfashionable backwater would not be one of his stylish haunts—but he just nodded.

'Sorry if it's out of your way,' she said stiffly as they entered the stream of bumper-to-bumper cars that he had explained away by saying *the bridge was closed*. He didn't appear to notice that she was being frosty so it seemed a wasted effort to be aloof.

She didn't ask what bridge. She found sharing the enclosed space with this man—the kiss still fresh in her mind—as mentally uncomfortable as the seat was physically comfortable. It didn't come as a shock. She had expected it. It was as if his personality was too big to fit in the small space, and she was coping, almost convincing herself that she was fine with it by the time they arrived outside her building.

She closed her eyes as he backed the long gleaming car, too quickly for comfort, into an impossibly narrow space in front of the purpose-built and boring beige-brick three-storey building.

'I won't be long,' she promised.

He watched her struggle with the belt for a moment then leaned in and pressed a button. For a few seconds his arm confined her to her seat, not that she could have moved. He pulled away a little but before she could breathe a sigh of relief he turned his head. He was so close she could feel the warmth of his breath on her cheek and see the individual lines fanning out from the corners of his deep-set eyes. His eyes, which had been drifting across her own face, found and lingered on her mouth.

Her eyelids drifted half closed, her breath when it came was a weak breathy flutter that left her oxygen-deprived lungs hungry. Hunger was what she thought she glimpsed in his dark-sky eyes before his lashes came down and he leaned back in his own seat, pressing his head into the head rest for a moment before he turned.

'Do I not get an invite in?' He could not pass up an opportunity to see where she lived. Marco would expect no less.

There was something else besides the mockery in his voice that she chose not to investigate, instead she funnelled all her energy into forgetting that torrid moment that was probably not torrid at all. After all, he could make scratching his nose look sexy. There was no one around to witness a kiss so no reason to kiss her.

'No, I'll be quicker without an audience.'

He shrugged. 'We've got time.'

She gave a snort of disbelief. He'd changed his tune. 'Since when?'

'I've yet to meet a woman who can pack quickly.'

Her feet on the pavement after a very neat swivel, she turned back. 'You have—me,' she said with the utmost confidence.

She clenched her teeth as she heard his soft steps behind her, annoyed but not surprised. She could have asked him what part of no did he not understand but it would have been a total waste of breath.

'I don't need help or a stalker.' She pushed her way through the swing door into the communal lobby, adding, 'The lift doesn't work.' Without looking at him, she began to skip up the stairs.

Her obvious reluctance to allow him to see where she lived had sparked his interest. Was there something she was hiding?

A secret lover?

The thought left a sour taste, but she had left a sweet taste—

He pushed the hot memory away, but not soon enough to prevent the lick of heat that streaked down his front, pooling in his groin, which made it hard to tell himself how uninterested he was in how many lovers she had, secret or otherwise. He was not here to judge, he was here to observe and present facts to Marco, who could make his own judgment.

Rose was breathing hard by the time they reached her front door. He, of course, wasn't. Her hand shook slightly as she put the key in the lock. 'You can wait here,' she mumbled as the door swung in.

'Sorry, what was that?'

She turned around, exasperated, as he stepped in behind her, but the exasperation lurched towards panic. He was standing close… Her heart picked up pace as her head tilted back. She tucked a curl behind one ear and took a carefully casual step back.

'How many bedrooms do you have?'

'This is the bedroom, and living room, and kitchen,' she said defensively.

'There is no bed.'

She felt the blush run under her skin and walked across to her wardrobe. She was fine with her virgin status but she didn't want to advertise the fact by blushing when a man said bed.

All right, maybe she wasn't *that* fine. Her inexperience had become something of an encumbrance. When was the right time to own up to your inexperience? Hopefully she'd recognise the moment when it came.

Of course, she needed a potential lover first, but she could wait. The sort of real deep relationship she wanted didn't happen overnight.

'There is a bed,' she said, pretending calm. 'It pulls down from the wall. I just shift the table. Look,' she added crankily, 'do you want a lesson in how the other half lives or shall I pack?'

'It's very...neat.' It was the only positive thing he could think to say about the box-like space and he was not sure what the white walls and pale furniture said about her. All her personal effects seemed to be stowed out of sight, except the books that overflowed off some built-in shelves. He wasn't sure how interested or useful Marco might find the fact she had a weakness for thrillers and cookbooks.

Rose looked at him sharply.

Was he being sarcastic? She decided to give him the benefit of the doubt. 'It came furnished and the landlord won't let me paint anything, but it's a good location and in my price bracket, and there's no spare bedroom so my dad can't stay over.'

Her eyes widened as the last bit slipped out. This was one of the reasons her dad considered her a social liability. She'd ruined more than one of his scams by blurting out the truth at an inopportune moment and, while she was good at putting people at their ease, she was not good at being polite to men who looked at her boobs, not her face. As for when one *'important contact'* had put his hand on her knee, lucky for him she had drunk half the cup of coffee she had tipped in his lap.

'I like my own space and the alternative, on my salary, would be a flat-share. I'm too old for that.'

His eyes skimmed her smooth, youthful skin. 'Oh, yes, I can see that,' he mocked, but the joke was on him as he imagined seeing more, much more...and touching… His breathing slowed and his core temperature jumped.

The tension zinged into life out of nothing and, unable to hold his dark gaze, she looked away, a tingle under her skin.

'So do I, like space, I mean. Families can be a pain?' he probed, reminding himself belatedly of why he was here.

'Do you mind? I need to get to the…' He stepped aside to allow her access to the sliding shower-room door.

A moment later she emerged with a toilet bag and she stretched up to drag a small holdall off the top of a wardrobe. It was a big stretch and gave him an excellent view of her taut behind. She stretched a bit higher and he bit back a groan. The little sadist had to know *exactly* what that wriggle was doing to him, he decided cynically. No woman who looked like her could be oblivious to her power.

She huffed a little as she finally got a grip. 'I'll only be a minute now.'

It took actually five.

'I'm impressed, except you've forgotten your luggage.'

'No, I haven't,' she contradicted smugly, nodding to the holdall she was hugging against herself like a protective blanket.

His brows lifted. 'A woman who travels light. I'm impressed.'

She took the compliment, if that was what it was, but it wasn't actually deserved. Her wardrobe, out of necessity given the storage space, was pretty limited. Even if she had packed everything she owned she could have fitted it into one suitcase.

'We moved around a lot when I was growing up. I got used to packing.' Sometimes in the dark—a moonlight flit, her dad had called the occasions when they'd moved by cover of darkness before the landlord came knocking for his rent.

The small secret smile that tugged at her lips as she looked at him through her lashes was intriguing. 'So you are well travelled…?'

She gave a dry laugh. 'My father travelled. I stayed at home mostly.'

With her dad it was always good to have an exit strategy.

'With family…friends…?' he probed casually.

'I was not a child.' Though actually, of course, she had been.

'It sounds like your father had a high-powered job.'

Her eyes dropped. 'He is very…entrepreneurial. I might need to buy a swimsuit.'

Recognising the neat change of subject and her discomfort when it came to discussing her father, he nodded, wondering if that meant she was afraid of incriminating herself, or alternatively she was ashamed of him. 'You're good swimmer, then?'

She waited for him to follow her through the door before closing it. 'No, I stay in the shallows.'

'You're afraid of water?'

'Not at all, just of drowning.' She could feel his eyes on her as she walked to the staircase.

'You should learn to swim.'

'I had a lesson once.' Her dad had thrown her in the deep end.

Her expression was veiled but Zac sensed an untold story in her response. 'What happened?'

Rose stepped outside and walked towards the luxury designer vehicle, not the sort of transport you used if you wanted to fade into the background, but then, irrespective of his mode of transport, Zac wasn't a *fading* person.

'I didn't float,' she responded finally as she sank into the deep leather. 'But I like beaches,' she said as Zac slid in beside her, adding a defensive addendum. 'For my time off, if the sea is close enough…? I know I'm not on holiday, Mr Adamos,' she told him earnestly and tried not to inhale the clean male scent—unique and disturbing—he brought with him.

Zac's angular jaw line clenched as provocative images floated through his head, instigating a testosterone current that sent hardening heat through his body. For seconds primal instincts were in charge as he imagined in tactile detail her, sleek and wet, wading out of the waves. The images had reached the point where he had laid her down on the sand when he closed down the reel. Imagination was a great thing when you were in charge, which he told himself he was, at all times.

There was a long pause while he reached for his phone, not because he needed to use it but as a useful prop until he felt safe, conscious that any vehicle was only as safe as the person behind the wheel.

'Is it far?'

Rose waited, hoping he'd elaborate—she was naturally curious about where she would be staying—but he didn't.

She huffed out a little sigh. He still hadn't pulled away from the kerb and was looking intently at his phone. His focus made her envy his physical indifference to her presence, while she was feeling the weakening effects of being bombarded by the male magnetism that rolled off him in waves that ought, in a fair world, to be illegal.

Rose lapsed into silence, feeling the misery caused by her awareness of his sinful influence on her hormones compounded by the fact the painkillers she had taken earlier were wearing off.

Had she packed her prescription migraine meds? Rose was *almost* sure she had.

Another sigh made him turn his head to look at her pensive, pale, delicate profile. 'Is there something wrong?' he asked. Nothing that keeping her out of reach should not solve, he decided, sliding his phone into his pocket.

She shook her head, hating the breathless feeling she got when she looked at him and hoping that familiarity would breed contempt or at least immunity. If not, the next couple of weeks were going to be uncomfortable!

'You were frowning and doing a lot of sighing.'

'No, I…I'm fine.'

'That's a very aggressive *fine.*'

Rose, who had been aiming for firm, was startled. She had never been called aggressive before.

'Got a slight headache.'

He looked sceptical but didn't challenge her on it as he pulled out of the parking space.

CHAPTER SIX

IT WAS A fifteen-minute drive but a world away from her poky flat. She knew the iconic building, of course. It was hard to miss on the skyline. Occasionally she'd wondered about the people who lived there and now she knew who one of them was.

Of *course* he lived in the penthouse. She was not good with heights.

'You can open your eyes now.'

Her lips tightened at the amusement in his voice but she didn't respond until she had stepped safely out of the open doors. 'Glass, and it faces outwards. I don't like heights.' Close on the snapped comment she realised who she had aimed her snappy response at—her boss, who had already called her aggressive once.

He'd also kissed her, but not really.

'That is...'

'A conceit of the architect.'

She felt tense to be on the receiving end of his mockery, but his comment took the wind out of her sails. It wasn't until a door opened that she realised

the lift had deposited her directly into his home. She
was standing in a reception hall that looked large
until she entered the living space.

'This is Arthur.' The man who had opened the
door looked almost as out of place in the open-plan
minimalist splendour of a living area the size of a
football pitch as Rose felt. She was trying hard not
to stare at his characterful nose that had to have been
broken multiple times.

Her eyes were drawn upwards. The ceiling was
lofty and dominated by a stained-glass cupola that
suffused the room with a tinted light. The rest of
the decor by contrast was uniform shades of white.
It crossed her mind that if someone had sat down to
design a layout that was *not* child-friendly, this would
be it. Open-plan with steps—just made for a small
child to tumble down—designed presumably to sep-
arate the space into individual living areas. There
was a great deal of dazzling glass. Even the modern
sculptures were all hard edges. The scattering of art
on the walls could not harm a child, just give him
nightmares, or maybe that was just her? She averted
her gaze from one particularly gross example with a
shudder. Maybe it was meant to make a person shudder, maybe that meant it was a masterpiece, but she
would not personally like it on her wall.

Struggling to adjust to the room, Rose gave her
silent verdict. Impressive to look at but not exactly
cosy to live in—it took more than a few bright cush-
ions and throws to achieve that. Not that anyone's
asking, she mocked herself, hoping that his Greek

base would adapt more easily to child occupation. Not that she would be around when the baby became a toddler.

'Hello,' she said, wondering where this tough-looking member of the household fitted in, with his craggy face, and his track suit and trainers. She couldn't figure it out, then he smiled at her and it didn't matter. She instinctively warmed to him.

'Any questions and Arthur will know the answer, unless it is baby-orientated and then you are the expert.'

'So no pressure, then,' the other man murmured, mirroring her thoughts exactly as he exchanged a look with Rose while Zac vanished. 'This way, miss.'

'Rose,' Rose said, following him weighed down not just by the holdall slung across her shoulder but by her headache which was still in the bounds of tolerable.

If she relaxed it might go away?

She ignored the sarcastic voice of negativity in her head that pointed out this hope was an exercise of optimism over experience.

'Shall I take that?'

Relieved of the bag, which though not bulky was heavy, she gave a grateful smile, not questioning her over-my-dead-body stubborn refusal to relinquish it when Zac had made the same offer on the way up from the car park.

'Thanks.'

'I had the bed made up in this room.' He pushed open a door that led into a room that was very five-star hotel, and placed her bag on the floor beside a queen-sized bed. 'Would you like to freshen up or…?'

'No, I'd like to meet the baby?'

He nodded and waited for her to walk past him. 'The nursery is just across here. The nanny was in the adjoining room but if you leave this door open you'll still be able to hear him…plus the room is Bluetoothed for sound.'

Something in his expression made her smile and speculate. 'He has good lungs?'

'I've heard quieter Harriers. Give me a nice peaceful war zone any day.'

'Jump jets…the vertical ones…?' She threw him a quizzical look. *'Air force?'* It would make sense. He had a definite military air about him.

He looked mock offended. 'Navy.'

Rose smiled back, wishing she could feel such an easy rapport with his boss…her boss too. 'Sorry.'

'Janet agreed to hold on until you arrived and I'll drop her at the airport on my way.'

'You are leaving?' That would mean… Rose pulled in a deep breath, mocking the thud of her traitorous heart and ignoring the quiver of illicit excitement low in her belly.

She wasn't alone. She had a baby to care for and for all she knew Zac—*Mr Adamos*, she self-corrected—having decided to keep things formal, professional, might not be spending the night alone either. There might be scarily clad supermodels drifting around the place.

One thing was certain—they definitely wouldn't be alone together!

'I'm heading out to Greece ahead to make sure everything's ready.'

'So you're a sort of…troubleshooter.'

'As good a word as any, a multitasker, that's me. It's hard for ex-servicemen to fit into civilian life. I was lucky, I've been working for Zac since I was invalided out… PTSD,' he added very matter-of-factly. 'I met him at a day centre the Adamos Foundation runs for ex-servicemen. There was a slight contretemps between a couple of guys, which I…*smoothed* over.'

He didn't detail what the smoothing had involved but Rose assumed it helped if your powers of diplomatic persuasion were backed up by muscle.

'Zac said he could do with someone like me, and it turned out he was right. OK, then,' he added in a stage whisper, 'this is the nursery.' They entered a room that was softly lit, the blinds drawn. Rose walked over to the cot. 'I'll leave you to it. Tell Janet I'm waiting when she's ready.'

'He's beautiful,' Rose whispered, looking down at the sleeping baby with a head of dark curls, his equally dark lashes resting like a fan against his flushed baby cheeks. 'Hello, Declan.'

'It's OK.' The Scottish-accented voice at her elbow was pitched at a normal volume. 'He won't wake. I know, famous last words, but really he's flat out. The poor wee thing has had a rough few days— colic, but it seems to have settled. You must be Rose.

I'm Janet. Do you mind if I give you the tour straight away? My mum's had a fall and fractured her hip. She's booked into surgery later today. I want to be there when she wakes up from the anaesthetic.'

'Of course. I'm so sorry about your mum.'

The tour was speedy but comprehensive and the other woman requested her email address and sent over some detailed notes she had made, which Rose accepted with gratitude.

'I've put a routine there but basically I've been playing it by ear until he settled, poor mite. You know the story?'

Rose nodded, feeling her throat thicken. 'The basics.'

'What a start in life!'

The kitchen was last on the whirlwind tour. Gleaming and high-tech, it was gadget heaven. Janet showed Rose where the formula was and explained, as she opened the massive fridge, that Arthur cooked.

'So I've been spoilt but he's left something for you to just pop in the microwave. You're only here the one night?'

Rose nodded, relieved when she didn't immediately regret it—fingers crossed this meant her headache was on the way out. It looked as if she could get away without taking the prescription meds, which she only resorted to when nothing else worked.

'I think so. Does Mr Adamos…do you eat with him?'

The woman laughed. 'Heavens, no, he's barely

seen the baby—' her tight-lipped disapproval showed '—let alone me. He eats out most nights, treats the place like a hotel…though with you…?'

Embarrassed by the speculation in the stare, Rose gave a carefully casual shrug and didn't pretend to misunderstand what she was hinting at. 'I really don't think I'm going to get mistaken for one of his girl-friends any time soon, do you? I doubt that I'll see any more of him than you have.'

I hope, she thought fervently as she tucked her crossed fingers into her pocket, though she didn't as yet share the other woman's disapproval. People reacted to bereavement differently and the baby had to be a reminder of a loss he might still be coming to terms with.

'Sorry,' the other woman said with a grimace. 'But you're such a pretty girl.'

'Well, I don't know the man *personally*.'

Could a kiss be classed as impersonal?

'I doubt that is going to change,' the woman re-sponded, her attitude perceptively warmer now that Rose was established as one of *the workers* and not one of the girlfriend class. 'I've barely exchanged two words with him. He hasn't been into the nurs-ery once. He communicates via Arthur.'

Rose arranged her features into a suitably sympa-thetic expression while thinking that the two-word limit had not stopped the older woman passing judg-ment.

'People react to loss differently…' He might be dealing with grief in his own way, and that grief might involve eating out in posh restaurants with beautiful women every night—who was she to judge?

Janet conceded this with a slightly grudging, 'You're right, I know. It's just my friends were so excited, jealous when I got the job…but I told them the nanny never gets the man.'

Not *this* man, Rose thought, feeling a wave of sympathy for the other woman who, despite her denial, had obviously built a few castles in the air around her employer…something easily done.

Her own fantasies were under control and she intended it to stay that way. An invite into his bed… she'd sooner accept an invitation to put her hand in the fire. In the long run it would be the less painful option, she decided, feeling a touch more positive because she hadn't allowed an image of his face to materialise in her head and she hadn't thought about the animal magnetism that rolled off him for at least five minutes.

She really hoped she would see as little of him as her predecessor.

Rose remembered that wish when she was alone later that evening. The apartment was so vast that it would have been easy to forget that there was anyone else there, except the somebody was Zac Adamos and he was not so easy to dismiss.

Up to that point there had not been too much time to think. She had kept herself busy familiarising herself with where the various baby essentials were kept, and after a debate it hadn't seemed worth unpacking her own things just for a night.

That headache that had lulled her into a false sense of security crept up on her just as the baby stirred… She sighed, as daggers stabbed her temples. The painkillers would have to wait.

Before he had left Arthur had said he'd keep Zac abreast of the arrangements and any potential issues that cropped up once he landed, but he did not foresee any problems.

On *that* count Zac had no worries, but as he sat in his book-lined, utterly silent library his focus was shot to hell! He'd not been able to work with the noise of a fretful baby and now it would seem he couldn't work without it—that really would be the supreme irony.

He was curious as to how she had calmed the child, but he had no intention of investigating. He saw no reason to revisit his decision to keep her at arm's length, preferably farther, the fact he really didn't want to proof that he needed to.

He turned back to the blank screen on his laptop, rose impetuously to his feet, changed his mind halfway to the door and, turning full circle, ended up at the built-in sliding cupboard containing some rather fine brandy… Hell, the redhead or parenthood or both is turning me to the bottle, he mocked himself as he poured a measure of the amber brandy into a glass. He held it but didn't drink, instead he found himself staring at liquid the colour of Rose's eyes.

He realised what he was doing and, choking out a snort of self-disgust, downed it in one. In the normal run of things this was a situation that would be easily remedied by scratching the itch… Sex was a great mind-clearer, not a solution available to him in this instance, so he might as well get drunk or at least get not totally sober!

Before he had time to put this plan into action there was a knock on the door.

It was no surprise to see who was standing there, it was a surprise to see how ill she looked.

'Theos!' he exclaimed, taking in her drawn ashen face, the bruised shadows under her eyes. 'You look terrible!'

Through the miasma of pain in her head Rose clutched at some bitterness. Did he think she needed telling this?

'Be fine in a minute now that I've thrown up.' Too much sharing, said her inner voice. Verbal shorthand was useful and quicker than full sentences when it took so much effort to get the words out. 'Saw a light under the door.' She was seeing lights now, ones that were not there in several colours zigzagging with dizzying intensity across her vision. It didn't distract her from the knives in her head. 'I'm s-sorry, but if you have any painkillers I forgot…' Her voice trailed away as she closed her eyes and pressed her fingers to her temples. 'Got a migraine.'

'You've got a *headache*?'

'No, I've got a bloody migraine!' She stopped and clutched her head, paying heavily for the yell as she swayed before adding in a whisper, 'Have to get back to the baby. He will need a feed.' She couldn't tell if the noise was part of the pain pounding in her skull or the baby crying. 'Can you turn the light off?' she pleaded, holding up a shaking hand to shade her eyes as she squinted up at him.

Swearing, he did just that and she sagged with relief.

'I'll call a doctor.'

'No…no… I just need a…'

He watched her sway like a sapling in the wind and then very gently crumple in slow motion. He caught her just before she reached the floor.

'Can you hear me? What do you need?'

Her head was against his chest. She squeezed her eyes closed. 'Not ambulance, painkiller and dark. I just need to close my eyes for a minute, then I can ch-check the baby.'

'I'll check the baby,' he said, sounding a lot more positive about his ability to do this than he felt. 'Piece of cake.'

'Shh!' she begged as agonising fire lit behind her eyes. 'No shouting!' she pleaded and pushed her face hard into his chest.

Startled by her action, Zac looked down at the fiery hot curls spilling down his front. She made a whimpering noise. The sound froze him to the spot as for a split second pure panic bolted through him, and something close to tenderness followed by a surge of protectiveness he refused to own.

She wanted to say, 'I'll be all right in a minute if

I can just stay here.' She managed a slurred, 'Just...'
Then without warning her knees sagged and gave,
and she began to slide.

'Hey there, I'm up here.'

She let the hands on her waist take the strain, relieved to have the task of standing upright taken out
of her hands. Her entire focus was on the hammers
inside her head and the ever-tightening band across
her forehead and behind her eyes. She told herself
that this wouldn't last for ever, that it would go away,
but it was little comfort.

She seemed oblivious when he scooped her up and
carried her to her bedroom, pulling the quilt back before he laid her down. Her knees immediately came
up to her chest. As he looked down at her lying there
shaking, he felt something move in him...something
that he refused to recognise as tenderness. He tried
hard to push the feeling with no name away, but it
held on tight, digging deeper until it felt like a fist in
his chest, tightening... She looked so damned *fragile*. He swore.

He was not her protector, he was Marco's friend.
As he wondered if he could feel any more conflicted
than he did she whispered, *'Sorry,'* and he had his
answer.

With a forearm pressed over her eyes she made
noise that he correctly translated as a request to draw
the blinds.

The darkness was bliss punctuated by pain. Rose
hated feeling vulnerable, she hated asking for help
with anything, but as the tears of weakness and pain

began to seep through her closed eyelids she swallowed her pride and whispered, 'Shoes...' A part of her frazzled brain knew she ought not to be giving him orders, but the knowledge slipped away as she was hit by a fresh wave of agony.

She barely registered him unlace her trainers or remove the zip-up cardigan she wore over a lace-edged vest. It might have been a minute later or an hour when he urged her to swallow some water to wash down the generic painkillers he'd emptied every drawer in his own bedroom to find.

'The baby?' she fretted. The idea of abandoning Declan made her half rise before she sank back... Rose knew what it felt like to be abandoned. It gave them a connection. She had felt it the moment she saw him.

The response came, soothingly competent and calm-sounding, which he *hadn't* been when he had forced himself to walk into the nursery. Next time it would be easier—he hoped.

'I looked in on him, he was asleep.' It had come as a relief to Zac, who had built up a picture in his head of accusing baby eyes looking up at him and seeing through his pretence, seeing he was not a fit guardian.

Holding his breath, he had searched the sleeping baby's soft features, trying to see a resemblance to the parents he had lost and failing, when something had broken free inside him. Suddenly he had understood how parents gave their lives for their children.

'You go to sleep too.' Declan wasn't her child, but

Rose had been willing to crawl to get to the baby. He pulled the cover up over her narrow shoulders and felt the same thing with no name move in his chest—it hurt.

If his last physical hadn't put him in the red zone of supreme fitness he might have been typing in his symptoms alongside his current Internet enquiry on migraine.

The volume of information when he had typed in his migraine query hadn't made him feel any less helpless. It was hard to pick the relevant facts out of the vast amount of information available. Helpless was something that Zac, a man of action and positivity, was not used to feeling.

There were some magic-sounding pills but as he didn't have access to them that wasn't much use. He'd rung his personal physician but had got the answer machine and an alternative number if this was an emergency. Zac had got frustrated and hung up in disgust. Should medics be allowed to have down time? At that moment he didn't think so!

'Can I do anything?' She looked so desperately ill that he struggled to believe that this was a migraine. He'd give it another thirty minutes and if she was no better he was calling an ambulance no matter what she said—not that she seemed capable of saying much.

'Distract me…' she mumbled.

He sat on the edge of the bed, his hand inches above her bright halo of hair, afraid to stroke her head in case he hurt her. Hurting a woman even accidentally was something that his entire being rejected, viscerally rejected.

'How?' Remembering her previous request, he kept his voice low.

'Talk about something nice.'

Nice... Hell, she wanted him to tell her a bedtime story! 'I don't know any stories.'

'Your Greek house, your family lived there...?'

Was she imagining a heritage that went back years? Nothing could be farther from the truth. Kairos, the man he considered his father, was a self-made man, not sentimental or resentful about his humble origins, and his mother's family had been hippies, her bohemian colourful antecedents had lived a gypsy lifestyle, colour, style, but no money.

They had both thought it odd when he took on the project of a fallen-down, derelict, formerly grand Greek stone house. What did he need a massive place in the middle of nowhere for? Was he planning to start a family? Kairos had joked.

Zac had been unable to explain even to himself. It had made him feel less sceptical when people spoke of instant connections after he experienced the strange sense of familiarity when he had stumbled on the place. The determination to bring it back to life had consumed him.

His family had speculated, the conclusions ranging from he'd lived there in a previous life—from his half-sister, deeply into crystals; he recognised a good investment—Kairos. Any financial gain had been accidental and his mother's suggestion he was looking for a baby substitute had turned out to be somewhat ironic considering he now had an actual baby.

'It's not a family home, it was a wreck that hadn't been lived in for years when I bought it...'

'Family?'

'I have a mother, a stepmother, she's Norwegian, and four stepfathers, also three half-sisters and four stepsisters,' he listed, and realised that he had gifted this woman he had known mere hours, and who he was meant to be surveying for character flaws, more personal information than he had trusted anyone with previously.

He hadn't even been aware of lowering his previously impregnable privacy barriers. How had that happened? he wondered as he watched her pale lips move in a faint smile, which he took to be a promising sign.

'So many...can I borrow one?'

He stood there in the dark and silence hearing the wistfulness in her voice. Marco or no Marco, at that moment if she hadn't drifted off to sleep he'd have told her.

Leaving her sleeping, he returned to the nursery. This time it was easier to make himself walk inside and this time when he walked to the cot he found it easier to look at the baby.

He was not asleep and his eyes were open. There was no accusation in them, just trust. Zac swallowed past the aching occlusion in his throat. They were Liam's eyes.

CHAPTER SEVEN

WHEN ROSE WOKE she didn't have a clue where she was, then suddenly it all came flooding back. She shot upright in bed, checked her head was still where it should be and sighed. Other than a muzzy feeling the pain was all gone.

Not the deep embarrassment. A second later as her thought processes cleared the embarrassment was overwhelmed by dismay! *The baby!* He had been her responsibility and she had dumped him on Zac. Gnawing worriedly on her lower lip, she slid off the bed and, not bothering to put on her shoes or run her fingers through her hair, dashed across the hallway to the nursery.

The blinds in the room were still drawn so she switched on the light and ran to the cot—the *empty* cot. Trying to stay calm, she ran towards the living area, and, exploding into the room, she stopped dead.

In a cream swivel chair Zac Adamos sat, a baby lying on his chest. The empty feed bottle on the side table spoke volumes.

They were both fast asleep.

Rose swallowed past the emotional lump in her throat. Both looked cute in *very* different ways. All right, Zac did not look cute, he looked quite unbelievably off-the-scale sexy with his tousled hair, stubble shadow emphasising the sharp angles of his face, and half-buttoned shirt revealing a slab of golden glowing skin. His relaxed sleeping face seemed younger.

Stepping over a trail of discarded ripped disposable nappies, she picked her way across the room to them. Closer, it was even more obvious that Zac, the urbane, sleek, perfectly groomed Zac, looked wrecked, admittedly a very sexy wrecked. His hair was standing up in spikes, his shirt sleeves were rolled up. Her eyes drifted as though drawn by a magnet to the section of deep toasty gold hair-roughened chest.

As she was staring his eyes opened.

'Good morning.'

She started guiltily. 'Good morning,' she whispered back, suddenly ridiculously shy. Last night they had stepped outside their designated roles and going back felt harder than it should have…

Would have helped if you'd combed your hair, Rose.

'I'm so sorry. I'm better now. I don't get them very often.'

'I am glad to hear that…' Presumably checking out her claim, he subjected her to a head-to-toe sweep, his conclusion hidden as his lash-shielded gaze was directed at the top of the sleeping baby's head.

Probably too polite to say she didn't look it, Rose decided, dragging a hand rather pointlessly through her hair. Not that so far he'd displayed much of that sort of restraint—he seemed a man who favoured calling a spade a spade, though when you were him there were no repercussions for being forthright. Nobody was going to cancel Zac Adamos and if they did, she doubted he'd care.

She watched as he shifted his position, sliding up in the chair as he flexed the fingers on the arm that was supporting the baby. 'I think my arm has gone to sleep…'

'Here, let me take him.' She bent towards him and held her arms out. As she eased the baby carefully from his chest, for a moment their eyes connected and the air buzzed with something that she refused to acknowledge as she broke the contact.

Pretending something wasn't happening got bad press but Rose was all for it. She positively embraced it!

He inhaled as she bent forward, her hair brushing his face, and Zac thought about it brushing his chest as she sat astride him. He was glad that the baby was there to bring some reality to the situation.

Lifting the baby into her arms jolted free the memory of him lifting her into his arms last night. Not much jolting was required—the memory was very close to the surface.

Equally easy to access was the strength of his arms, the warm solidity of his body something to cling to as the pain sucked her into her own private hell.

Her nostrils flared as she relived the moment

minus, luckily, the pain, but with the warm male scent of him.

The blurred memories of the attack were sharpening with each passing second. She knew from experience that some would be lost for ever, but the ones that were not lost were making her squirm with embarrassment. Her boss had put her to bed, and, as if that weren't crossing enough professional boundaries, she'd asked him about his family.

He had told her.

Zac watched her settle the baby on her shoulder, his face nuzzling into her neck. She made it look so easy but he knew it was not.

'Have you been there all night?' The idea of him sleeping in a chair with the baby made emotions clutch in her chest.

'He fell asleep and I didn't want to risk waking him.'

'You fed him?'

'I would claim it was easy,' he said, levering himself into an upright position.

Rose watched, a worried corner of her brain noting the inescapable element of compulsion about her hungry scrutiny. But he made easy watching, she decided as he pressed one hand to the bottom of his spine and raised the other above his head to sinuously stretch out the kinks before he proceeded to rub a hand vigorously back and forth across his dark hair, creating a sexy mess.

Observing the effect, Rose wondered if the women he woke up with speared their perfectly manicured fingers into those ebony strands as they kissed their way down the column of his neck to his chest... Catching a sharp little breath, she applied the emergency brakes to the illicit scene playing in her head before it became personal.

'So how did you?'

'Cope...? I rang my mother, who talked me through the process. Once she had stopped laughing,' he added darkly, thinking of the conversation he'd had with his parent, trying to make himself heard above a baby's hungry screams.

This entire scene was so unimaginably impossible that Rose laughed too, then realised who she was laughing at, and stopped. The events of last night seemed to have significantly blurred the lines of their employer-employee relationship, a blurring that for her had started when he'd kissed her.

Was she imagining an intimacy that didn't exist?

'The one with four husbands?' The words were out before she could stop them. It was the sort of spontaneous stupidity that a person blurted out when they were not fully awake and their brain was still playing catch up.

'She only has one at a time and the last one appears to be a keeper,' Zac observed, watching the baby nuzzle her neck. It was an image that gave him chest pain again. The sensation was not one he embraced. 'She is a big believer in if at first you don't succeed, try, try and try some more.'

Rose, shifting her weight from one foot to the other, could only assume this family-orientated person would disapprove of a nanny literally sleeping on the job. How much influence did she have with her son…enough to get Rose sacked?

And who could blame her? Rose thought. She had not exactly covered herself in glory so far, but she really didn't want to lose this job, she decided fiercely. She didn't want to miss the chance to see Greece.

Nothing at all to do with the man who had just risen to his feet looking like a ruffled sex god.

Oh, no, Rose, nothing at all.

'I didn't mean to be… You told me about your family last night,' she finished on an awkward rush.

'Ah, your little bedtime story. Sometimes fact is stranger than fiction.'

'I don't really remember.' She wasn't sure she imagined that he relaxed slightly at her lie. 'But I do want to thank you. I'm very sorry I was such a… nuisance.'

He moved towards her at an immediate physical disadvantage due the disparity in their heights, and she felt her heart quicken. The baby on her shoulder stirred as her grip tightened slightly around his warm body.

'Hush,' she murmured, brushing his soft cheek with her lips. The baby's presence felt a protective shield, whether from his guardian's disturbing high-voltage presence or her own bewildering feelings around him. Both possibilities were equally confusing.

Her mouth ran dry as their glances connected. The contact lasted a second before he was rubbing a hand down his stubble-roughened jaw line, no doubt thinking of nothing more sexy than a shave and shower, she mocked herself. The rest was in her head. The knowledge didn't stop her tipping over into babble-inducing panic mode.

'Was your mother shocked?' *Horrified*, she tacked on silently, at the very least *not happy*. Her son demanded the extra mile from all his staff, why should the mother be any different? Though in this instance the son was being quite surprisingly understanding for a man who had spent the night in an armchair with a baby, afraid, as far as she could tell, to move a muscle. His reputation was not one of patient understanding, fair but tough.

'Less shocked, more—' He hesitated, the indent between his dark brows deepening as he recalled her comment... *'You need my help? That's a first, darling.'*

'My mother is not really shockable.'

He'd last seen her at the funeral, along with her present husband of ten years. Guy had lost more hair and the age difference was a lot less obvious. Guy was ten years older than Liam, who never got to worry about a receding hairline or hear his baby's first word.

Rose observed the fading of his half-smile and for a moment she glimpsed emotions that were more layered and complex. But before she could begin to interpret them the effective shield of his ebony lashes came down in what she understood as a 'subject closed' action, so she was surprised when he supplemented his original comment.

'She is still shaken by the death of Liam and Emma. Liam was a scholarship boy at my boarding school. Being in foster care, he used to spend holidays with us. She used to say she wished I was more like him.' Liam had always been more tactile and demonstrative than Zac was growing up.

'She struggles with unhappy endings.' Even though they were the norm in life. 'In my mother's world true love always leads to a happy ending.' The harsh cynicism in his voice made Rose wince in silent protest. She had a fondness for happy endings herself, though as yet not much first-hand experience of them. 'A prime example of stubborn optimism over experience considering her track record,' he mused.

'Is she not—' She stopped, bit her lip and apologised, cursing her runaway tongue.

'Yes, she is happy, my mother is a great believer in the power of love and an equally strong proponent of family and marriage. She believes in it so much so that…well, I have three half-sisters.'

'I know,' she began, and stopped, remembering too late she had claimed amnesia when actually she remembered every word he had said. His voice had been an anchor to cling to in a sea of pain. She smiled and lifted a hand to her head. It was so very good not to hurt.

'You still have a headache,' he accused, picking

up on the gesture. She was finding it was worrying just how much he noticed.

'No, I'm fine.' She produced a slightly manic smile to prove the point and turned the subject. 'Was your father, was he her first—' Turned in the wrong direction. It was immediately obvious even without the frost in the air that she'd hit a nerve. Her dad had once called her a social liability and he wasn't far out in this instance. 'Sorry, that was—'

'Clumsy, yes. She did *not* marry my father. He is dead.'

If she had felt bad before, now she felt mortified. 'I'm so sorry.'

He looked at her curiously. On most people's tongues the trite phrase was meaningless, but Rose meant it. Her sincerity was not in question, but his sanity was.

He had been cornered by the slickest of clever interviewers, every variation of every trick, surprise, ambush, flattery, had been tried, but he had never discussed his biological father, never revealed even a snippet of information, not even that he knew his identity. He'd never given even the smallest foothold to provide them with leverage, not even a *no comment*. To his knowledge only he, Kairos and his mother knew the man's true identity, who and what he had been.

Zac's biological father had been what *he* was never going to be, a weak, abusive bully, which was why he was never going to oblige his mother by marrying or having children. Why risk passing on his tainted genes to another generation?

This redhead, who wore her emotions so close to the surface it must *hurt*, had achieved what no experienced investigative journalist had and, with no pushing or coercion, he had voluntarily given out information.

He was stone-cold sober so he didn't even have that excuse!

Ironically the recipient was oblivious to what she had been handed, but even if she had known he was certain she would not have used it.

Or could it be an act? Just because she seemed to have dragged some hidden weakness of his own to the surface, he owed it to Marco to consider this possibility. Could she just be very good at pulling strings? His jaw flexed, the fine muscles quivered, growing taut at the idea of anyone pulling *his* strings. In his view it made sense to be wary especially of something that was too good to be true, and he could see for some Rose Hill might fill that brief—she *was* too good to be true, all warmth, sincerity, beauty, a hint of fire and blazing sensuality.

He'd see this thing through even though he suspected his report to Marco would be short and boring, but this wasn't the moment to go with his gut instincts. If he was wrong, if he made the wrong call, it was Marco and Kate who would suffer.

He knew that part of the reason Marco had tasked him with finding out if Rose was one of the good guys or her father's daughter was not just because of their friendship but because it would not have crossed his old friend's mind that Zac would be anything less than objective. Emotions wouldn't cloud his judgment.

Zac would not have questioned his ability to deliver this objectivity, even given the lust factor, *before* he saw her willing to drag herself to the baby's side when she was in agony, before she shook loose feelings that he still couldn't bring himself to acknowledge.

It would be easy for him to say case closed right now, and tell Marco you got exactly what you saw: the face of an angel with the lush lips of a sinner… missing out the part that she heated his blood like no woman he'd ever encountered.

The other option was that she was the best actress who'd never won an Award! But last night's pain had stripped away any defences she possessed, her total vulnerability exposed, and Zac had never felt so *protective*. There was a part of him that wanted to discover a dark secret, that wanted her *not* to be genuine. He'd been in her company for only a matter of hours but his gut instinct was telling him she was authentic…his gut or was that other parts of his anatomy talking?

He nodded his head in mocking gratitude. 'A lot of water under the bridge. My mother married Kairos, who is my stepfather. They co-parented me, but he's not my father, which is one of the world's most shared secrets,' he drawled.

'Not by me.'

Some of the tension that had crept into the room, fuelled by undercurrents she was aware of but didn't understand, faded at her retort. 'Good to know that my secrets are safe with you.' He hesitated a moment. 'You said it doesn't happen often?'

'No, really, it won't happen again. It's rare I have a full-blown attack like that. I usually catch it in time. There are warnings sometimes…an aura…some visual disturbances,' she explained, seeing his blank look.

'But not always a warning,' he persisted.

'I have never missed a day's work because of it.'

Zac fought the urge to correct her assumption that he was speaking as an employer, not someone who was concerned.

Why wasn't he speaking as an employer?

'I have no doubt,' he drawled. It was easy to imagine her dragging herself into work with a broken leg. She was a stubborn little thing with a martyr complex stamped into her DNA. 'I knew about migraine but I never knew it could be so incapacitating.'

She could hardly deny that, because she *had* been incapacitated. After trying to hold it together she'd just let go, and he'd been there to catch her—quite literally. Her eyes slid to his big hands and her insides quivered. Conscious of the strange ache in her chest, she remembered taking comfort in his strength, but it was the gentleness that had stayed with her.

'A lot of people have it worse.'

Remembering her lying in the foetal position, her

eyes tight shut, overwhelmed with pain, Zac struggled to believe that was possible.

'I'm not sure what the schedule for today is? But if it's not too inconvenient, I could pick up my medication from my flat just in case… Is it on the way to the airport?' She waited, not looking directly at him, ready for him to tell her he'd made other arrangements—someone who wasn't likely to fall down on the job quite literally.

'A detour is no problem. It would be a lot more inconvenient if that happened again.' He might as well play the heartless employer if that was what she thought him… Besides, it was not so far from the truth. He was a good employer for practical reasons not sentiment. People who were happy in work were more productive, it was logical.

What was not logical was imagining even for a moment holding her while she slept…scooping her body against his, not in a sexual way, even though she lit fires inside him he hadn't known were there. Last night he had experienced an utterly alien need to comfort her.

The recollection was one he pushed away as he reminded himself he was a man who headed for the hills at the first sniff of neediness in a woman, a woman who wanted more than he was willing or able to give.

The baby in Rose's arms started squirming. She looked down with a smile. His eyes were screwed up and he had shoved his fist in his mouth.

'So I still have a job?' It was only half a joke.

'Did you think otherwise?'

'You offered to sack Andy... And your reputation...' She stopped, flushing, wondering when she was going to stop putting her foot in where angels feared to tread... The mixed-up narrative in her head represented her tangled emotions.

'Please don't stop. You were just getting educational. I'd be fascinated to learn what reputation I have.'

'All right then, ruthless. I didn't say I believe them,' she added.

'Because you think the best of people?' he drawled, thinking she was the living, breathing definition of a lamb to the slaughter.

'He's waking. I need to feed him,' she said, dodging his eyes and the question as little Declan provided a god-sent distraction from a fresh surge in tension that seemed to spring into life at regular intervals when they were sharing a space. 'Come on, sweetheart, let's get you sorted,' she crooned, beginning to jiggle him in her arms. She took a step and turned back. 'What time are we leaving?'

'When you're ready.' Zac had a new and, for someone who took for granted his ability to learn new tasks easily, very real appreciation of how a baby's needs were time-consuming.

'I'll be as quick as I can,' she promised, determined to make up for last night.

She needed to show him that she really wasn't the weakest link. She'd been looking after herself most of her life—all of her life—but last night someone had been there for her. Zac had been there for her.

What would it be like to have someone there when you needed them, someone who *wanted* to be there, wanted to protect you, someone to share the good times and the bad…share a family…? Would she ever know? she wondered wistfully.

'The kitchen, it might be…sightly messy… I was looking for…things…'

It was an afterthought that mystified Rose—it was his kitchen, after all—but when she walked into the room, the tinge of something close to embarrassment made perfect sense. *Slightly* messy did not cover it. The place looked as if a bomb had hit it, cupboards and drawers open, the work surfaces cluttered with their contents.

She cleared enough of the mess to be able to prepare the baby feed, while nudging the baby in his rocker chair with her foot.

Zac made a few calls and checked his emails, and made a few Internet face-to-face calls. The last-minute nature of the Greek trip had involved his office making some major changes to his diary. The only one that he had refused to cancel was a dinner for a director who had been with the foundation since its inception and whose dedication and expertise, given freely, had gone a long way to its success. Charles deserved more than a handshake and he had plenty of gold watches.

Flying back to London for the event had seemed

the only realistic solution. It was one of his team who had suggested half jokingly that he could shift the party to Greece, fly everyone out and make a weekend of it.

The idea had appealed to Zac and he had set the plan in motion.

After being holed up for an hour, when he left the room Zac was hit by the smell of coffee and a blissful silence. He resisted the coffee aroma, sent up a prayer of thanks for the silence and headed for the shower.

Zac's dark eyes squeezed closed as he lifted his head, enjoying being pummelled by the darts of hot steamy water ironing out the kinks in his spine left by the night he'd spent afraid to move in case the baby woke.

He found his thoughts turning to Rose's relaxed competence with the baby. He doubted he would ever feel relaxed. He doubted… He pushed the thoughts away but the insecurities lingered. At least the child did not have his DNA to deal with, he just had a parent who left a lot to be desired. He would never be able to fill Liam's shoes, he knew that. The loss of his friend lay like a cold boulder in his chest. Zac was determined to do his best, whatever that turned out to be, but for the first time in his adult life self-doubt plagued him.

He deliberately let the image of Rose's face float into his head and the rest faded away. She was the biggest problem of all and one, despite everything, he would have given a lot to enjoy. The fact he was even torturing himself with the possibility said how big his problem was.

CHAPTER EIGHT

HE TURNED THE shower to cold. The icy jets only partly solved his problem, which was that he wanted something that he couldn't have... Not complicated, Zac. The control that he had grown to take for granted was being challenged because he was allowing it to be, he told himself. He had to stop indulging in fantasies and fulfil his promise to Marco and get Rose Hill out of his life and reunited with the family she appeared to long for.

Rose, the baby tucked on one hip, was talking away as though the infant could understand every word as she set about the task of untangling the straps on a baby rocking chair. She didn't immediately realise that Zac had entered the room until his shadow fell across her.

'Oh, good,' she said, focusing on the practical use he could be and not how her stomach had gone into butterfly mode. 'Could you lend a hand with this? It's got in such a tangle.' She clicked her tongue in irritation.

Before he knew what she wanted—his thought

processes were a little slowed by the distraction of her behind encased in blue denim—she had got to her feet and thrust the baby at him.

'Could you? I need to use two hands.'

'What…?'

Rose watched as he looked at the baby as if it were an unexploded bomb. 'That's right, support the head…you've done it before, yeah, that's perfect. You're a natural,' she lied.

The pat-on-the-head lie made his jaw quiver. If he could have risked taking his eyes off the baby, he would have glared at her for daring to patronise him, a circumstance that should have made him more annoyed than he was.

Zac Adamos looking *almost* vulnerable, not arrogant and in control. Who'd have thought? she mused, fighting off a smile that faded of its own accord as the word *dangerous* floated into her head.

She shivered. 'You can breathe,' she offered in a tight little voice as she bent back to her task. The task she was getting paid for. Among all this domestic familiarity, it was good to remind herself of her position here.

The baby looked up at him with what Zac imagined was disappointment… Sorry, mate, Zac thought. You did pull the short straw.

'He's not crying.'

Rose straightened up. 'I can't take the credit. Janet said he had colic, poor scrap. She had had a tough few days, but he's feeling better—aren't you?' She moved in close, pursing her lips as she threw the baby a kiss and smiled.

Zac clenched his jaw at the resultant hormone surge he had zero control over and stood rigid as she took the baby from him. Some of the tension slid from his shoulders as he was relieved of the warm bundle and she stepped away, not far enough to stop his nostrils flaring in response to the scent of her shampoo, or was it just the scent of her?

'*Janet?*' he repeated, frustration and the irritation he felt with himself putting harshness in his deep voice.

She looked surprised by the question. 'Janet, my predecessor. Oh, her mother's op went very well...' She slung him a cheery smile over her shoulder as she crouched down to clip the baby in the chair, sounding as though she expected this to be good news to him.

'How on earth do you know that?'

'She texted me a few minutes ago.'

'You appear to have bonded.'

She straightened up. Maybe he was always this grumpy in the morning? Or maybe just on a morning after he had spent the night in a chair with a baby on his knee when he might have had other plans.

Aware of a simmering tension in the room, she tilted her head to meet his hooded dark stare and felt her stomach muscles twist.

She swallowed, looked away and took longer than necessary to dab the baby's drooly rosebud mouth with a muslin square. Better to face facts. If there was tension, it was in *her*, not the room.

She was attracted to him. She knew she was being faintly ridiculous, but it had been a lot easier when she was able to balance his expertise in the kissing department when he was the shallow, selfish boss with ice in his veins, a calculator where his heart should be... Some of the stuff people said about him had to be true.

She was clinging hard to the image of a callous charmer, which was not easy after the way he had looked after her last night and then this morning with the baby... She had to get a grip!

She felt dizzy when she thought about him kissing her. She *should* have felt disgusted, it had been so calculating. Instead she felt...she wasn't going to think about what she felt because with luck it would go away like her headache. She was not going to make the situation worse by making a total fool of herself by betraying what was a belated sexual awakening. *That* would be a blow she didn't think her pride could withstand.

'Are you packed?'

'Oh, yes, things are all sorted, Janet had done most of it before she left and I didn't unpack last night.'

'You can pick up your migraine medication on the way to the airport.'

'Thanks. She says that her mum's sister is coming over from Canada.'

The relevance of this information passed him by

until it dawned on him that she assumed that the previous nanny was coming back when her personal circumstances changed. He had no reason to correct her.

'Did you bring anything dressy?'

She stared at him, her smooth brow pleating at the question. 'I didn't think I'd be dressing for dinner...' Realising he might misinterpret her sarcasm, she added quickly, 'Declan is OK with informal.'

Rose extended her foot to gently rock the baby chair, smiling as the occupant began to kick his feet with uncoordinated enthusiasm.

'I just thought you might like to explore in your down time. There are some pretty nice places to eat. But no matter, you can buy what you need when you get there. Order anything you need. I've made arrangements for you to use my accounts.' When he'd made the arrangements it had seemed a good way to test her honesty or otherwise for Marco.

At what point over the last twenty-four hours had the idea stopped being a test of Rose's honesty and simply a convenience? He didn't know at what precise moment his suspicions had died a natural death, but, while she might have nothing to prove to him, Marco would no doubt be pleased when he was able to show him this further proof of her integrity.

Unless she cleaned him out and skipped the country?

Her attention swung from the baby to the man standing with his shoulders propped against the wall, his negligent stance in direct contrast to the intelligence glinting in his eyes and the air of barely suppressed energy that even a sleepless night hadn't put a dent in.

'I have everything I need,' she said, acting, to his amusement, as if he had just offered her an insult, not his trust.

'I don't need anything I can't buy myself.' Certainly not something you are paying for, she thought, before belatedly realising that she had jumped the gun. He hadn't been offering to buy *her* a wardrobe. Mortified by her error, she tacked on quickly, 'But yes, baby will need things, that will be useful. Is the house far from a town?'

'Aphrodite, my villa, is relatively remote. It is set in its own grounds, which guarantees privacy.'

Rose nodded. *She* had no concerns about isolation. She was excited about her first taste of foreign travel…and isolation had its positives. She had struggled with the decision but in the end she had not contacted her dad to tell him about her temporary move. She felt guilty but she knew that if her dad knew her place was empty, he'd offer to house-sit or, even worse, turn up in Greece and try to cadge a free bed.

'Won't the isolation make it hard for you to make your base there on a permanent basis?'

'There is such a thing as the Internet and I won't be there twenty-four-seven.'

'Obviously,' she said, even though actually it hadn't been that obvious to her. She'd be able to relax, she told herself, without his presence making her feel as though she were constantly walking a tightrope without a safety net.

'Athens is a thirty-minute helicopter transfer away and the flight into London is not exactly long haul.'

He spoke casually of helicopter transfers the way only the very rich did. 'You've thought of everything.'

She had to admire his commitment to the role that had been thrust upon him, to the extent that he was prepared to make such a major life change for the baby. But to her way of thinking interacting with Declan was more important than uprooting his life for the sake of the baby and maybe regretting the move.

Though what did she know? Maybe the timing was good and this wasn't just about the baby, maybe one of those long-legged beauties had pierced his reputedly stony heart and he'd already decided it was time for a lifestyle change?

Her lips twisted into a grimace as she masochistically dwelt on the image of his mouth losing its cynical twist and wearing an intimate smile as he looked at this faceless beauty that had captured his heart.

She pressed a hand to her stomach, and diagnosed the sensation—a touch of envy, yes, but not, obviously, of a woman who landed him.

He was easy to fancy, but living with him would be a nightmare. *Not that you're ever going to know, Rose*, mocked the voice in her head.

No, what she envied was simply the idea of being

part of a family, a *real* family. In her experience people who had them didn't realise how lucky they were.

Obviously it was a plus if a child could be brought up with space and freedom to thrive, but it wasn't about where a child lived. Her eyes flickered momentarily to the drooling baby and her expression softened. What any child really needed was a family... and love.

He glanced at his phone. 'The driver is here. Tell him where to stop off and I'll see you at the airport.'

'You're not coming w—' She stopped. Obviously he wasn't coming with them and she was in danger of sounding disappointed.

'I have a few things to sign off on. I'll see you there.' His eyes went to the baby. 'I'll see you both there.' After the shortest of hesitations he reached out and touched the baby's cheek.

'So soft,' he observed, sounding startled, before seeming to realise she was watching him and dropping his hand. On anyone else she would have called the expression on his face self-conscious.

Rose had no first-hand experience to compare with, but she was assuming that the sort of luxury, every-need-attended-to service she was enjoying was not available on a typical flight.

She had not been offered a menu but she had been asked what she would like. The attendant seemed confident whatever she requested the chef would be able to provide.

Thrown, Rose had resorted to asking what the young woman would recommend.

'The lobster is—'

'Fine, I'll have it.'

'The wine list?'

'No, I'll not have…' Actually, why not? This might be her only experience of flying in a private jet, she might as well enjoy it… Also, a glass of wine might unknot the tension in her shoulders, just the one. 'You choose.'

The lobster was melt-in-the-mouth and buttery and the wine did help her relax.

The only negative of the experience was not that Zac had not joined her—a little bit of delicate probing had revealed he was sitting upfront with the pilot—but the possibility that he might suddenly appear, which stopped her relaxing *enough* to enjoy the experience fully.

She was clipping on her seat belt for landing when Zac did appear, shrugging his jacket on as he walked towards her before flopping elegantly into the seat opposite her.

'Comfortable flight?'

'I've got nothing to compare it to, but I was well looked after.'

A look of shock crossed his face. 'You've *never* flown before?'

He couldn't have sounded more shocked if she had announced that she had come from Mars. She shrugged and wondered what his reaction would be if she admitted that she'd never been outside the UK before.

'But not your first time abroad? Your father never took you with him on his travels?'

'Not for business. I was at school, we moved around the country. When he went abroad… I was old enough to look after myself.'

How old did her father consider old enough? he wondered grimly—Zac had suspicions. He found he was envying Marco his opportunity to tell the man exactly what he thought about him when he warned him off. Zac would have enjoyed some warning of his own.

'That's pretty,' he observed. The upward curve of his lips distracted from the ice in his eyes as he stretched his hand towards the amber stone she wore suspended on a gold-coloured chain around her neck.

Rose's lashes fluttered before her eyes lifted to his face. 'Oh, yes…' She caught the stone in her fist, pressing the coldness into her palm. 'It was a birthday present from my dad…' She began and stopped, her smile fading.

It was a story she had trotted out so many times that she almost believed the lie herself. She began to shake her head, then laughed, an invisible tipping point reached. She just couldn't tell the pathetic lie again.

The truth was pathetic too but at least it was the truth. What was the point of perpetuating the pretence? She wasn't a child trying to fit in with the other kids who took for granted their birthday parties and gifts, who complained about curfews and being grounded…being *cared* for, not that they realised it. But Rose did because it was something she didn't have.

'No, no, that's not true. He didn't buy it for me. I bought it myself! I saw it on a market stall and saved up. I gave the stallholder a little each week until I could buy it for myself and I told… I pretended.'

There was a silence as he stared at her. She couldn't tell what he was thinking…but then she didn't want to. She lowered her gaze to her hands clasped on her lap. She didn't want to see his embarrassment or, worse, his pity.

She pressed a clenched hand to her mouth and thought, *A bit late*, as she shook her head. Her eyes above the hand were filled with tears and she wanted to die of embarrassment.

'You have excellent taste,' Zac observed, making no reference to her massive meltdown as he took hold of the pendant between his long fingers.

Her lowered eyes lifted. She didn't know what reaction she had expected but this hadn't been it.

He leaned in slightly and Rose fought the instinct to mirror his action as her nostrils twitched to the scent of the male fragrance he used…or maybe it was just him. 'It is…' he turned the pendant over in his hand '…Victorian?'

She looked at his sleek dark head shining blue black and wondered if it was as marvellously silky as it looked. 'I don't know, I just thought it was pretty.'

His eyes were on the stone and not her face. It gave Rose an opportunity to regain her composure and she was grateful for it.

'The smaller black stones around the amber are, I think, jet, though I am no expert on jewellery.'

Just how to pay for it, and not this sort of jewellery, she thought, polishing her cynicism.

'You delegate that task, do you?' She couldn't help herself or maybe she didn't try. His parting gifts to exes were the thing of legend in the Adamos building.

He let go of the pendant and pulled up straight, fixing her with a dark stare that glittered with humour.

The words *Can you see the Gorgeous Great White laughing at himself?* floated through her head… He could!

He was glad to see her biting her lip and looking guilty, not devastated. The look in her eyes as she'd told her story, the simplicity of the recounting, no play for sympathy, in fact actively rejecting sympathy, had touched him at a deep level that no one had ever reached before.

'Play nice, Rose. I was showing my sensitive side. Seriously though, I'm sorry you didn't get birthday presents…all children should,' he observed, keeping it light and hoping one day she would meet a man who would make up for all those lost birthdays… The thought of this man who would get to do this made him feel oddly dissatisfied.

'Did you?'

'Oh, yes… I still do. It doesn't matter how often I tell them I'm too old to celebrate birthdays, they keep sending me reminders of how old I am.'

'Of course, you're *never* too old to celebrate your birthday. I think everyone should have their birthday as a holiday. It should be written into law.'

He reached into his pocket, remembering the forgotten discarded home-made card that had escaped the bin. He'd stuffed it in his pocket, meaning to dispose of it. He got it out now and uncreased the folds before handing it to her.

'Oh, that's so sweet.' She looked up from the crayoned offering. 'Who is…Carla?' she asked, deciphering the lopsided name in front of the kisses.

'A niece.'

'How old is she?'

'I don't have a clue…but she can write…' he glanced at the card '…so she might be, what, five or thereabouts…?'

She laughed, assuming he was joking. 'You make fun, but it must *mean* something if you kept it.' He was not as heartless as he liked to make out.

He looked amused, a look, of course, which was very attractive on him. 'I hate to disillusion you, but I just forgot to bin it with the rest.'

Her face fell. She hated that this was something he found amusing. 'I hope you will celebrate Declan's birthday,' she said sternly, adding a self-conscious, 'Mr Adamos,' as an afterthought.

'Make it Zac. If I didn't give Declan a party with

all the bells and whistles I think his mum and dad would haunt me, *Rose*.'

She glanced from his sombre face to the sleeping baby, her heart aching when she realised she would never see any of his birthday parties. In a short space of time that little baby had burrowed his way into her heart. 'How…?' She stopped and shook her head. 'Sorry, you don't want to talk about it.'

'I haven't talked about it. The people at the funeral talked incessantly about the *tragedy*, but what they really meant was "I'm glad it's not me".'

'I suppose that's a natural reaction.'

'It's hypocrisy and—'

She watched as he clamped his white lips tight as if the physical action alone could hold the anger in. Rose was of the opinion he would be better off letting it out.

'It was a lorry,' he said abruptly. 'They were on their way from the hospital. Emma wanted to remain with the baby, but she was exhausted and parent accommodation on the SCBU was overstretched.'

'He was premature?'

He nodded. 'They never stood a chance. It went across the central reservation and hit them head-on. Dead instantly, the inquest said, like that was some sort of comfort.'

Rose didn't say anything, afraid that she would stop the flow of confidences.

'The driver had a heart attack but survived.'

'Poor man,' she exclaimed, eyes wide with horror, before catching Zac's expression and adding, 'To have to live with that knowledge must be terrible.'

'Too early for me to be philosophical. I think, to quote from the beginner's guide to bereavement and other equally useless books on the subject available, that I've moved from denial to anger.' He gave a bitter laugh. The stages of bereavement sounded so straightforward on the page of a book—in reality they were anything but.

'I've never lost anyone close,' she said quietly. Anything she said would come from a position of ignorance. 'But I'm a good listener...' The offer was there with the silent addition of no pressure.

The soft words brought his eyes to her face, her eyes wide and soft, her expression pensive as her teeth dug into her plump lower lip.

What is this? A therapy session?

His spine stiffened. For some bizarre reason he was indulging in some sort of soul-baring exercise instead of fulfilling his promise to Marco.

'I'll keep that in mind but if I feel in need of therapy I'll go *talk* to a professional.'

He saw the hurt in her eyes but didn't allow it to influence him. In his opinion if anyone needed talking therapy it was her. If she carried on leaking empathy the way she did she'd be drained dry before she was thirty.

'So your parents are alive?' he said, belatedly taking charge of the conversation.

'My dad is— Didn't I tell you this? He's alive, and I've no brothers or sisters.'

'Your mother?'

'She left…she didn't want me.' She blinked rapidly, her lashes quivering dark against her cheek, confused as to why she had told him that. She *never* volunteered information about the mother who walked away when she was a baby. 'That doesn't make me a victim,' she added quickly. 'Not all people are cut out to be parents… Oh, I didn't mean you.'

His bark of laughter dissolved some of the invisible tension that had built up. The half-smile that followed held no humour as he added in a hard voice, 'Why not? It's probably true.' His shoulders lifted in one of his inimitable shrugs. 'But I'm the only option Declan has. Let's hope I don't let him down.'

His comment opened up a range of possibilities that she had not considered. He seemed so impregnably confident that the possibility, no, *probability* that he could experience the same insecurities that anyone faced with parenting was surprising. Acknowledging he had weaknesses made things shift inside her in a way she couldn't explain even to herself.

'I'm sure every parent who brings a baby home feels the same pressure.'

Conscious of a sudden weariness, he ran a hand across his forehead almost expecting to discover lines gouged into his skin—he felt he'd aged half a lifetime in the last few weeks. 'Liam and Emma never got to bring their baby home, never got to worry.'

Her eyes misted as she leaned forward, her hands clasped tight in her lap. There were no words that would make the anger and pain she saw in his eyes go away. She wished there were. 'Life s-stinks s-sometimes!'

The hard lines on his face relaxed. If she had said the *right* thing, along the lines of *It gets better* or *Time heals* or any of the trite things that people said on such occasions he would have exploded. Instead her brutal honesty pulled him back from the brink of losing it.

'You won't get any arguments from me. You do realise that we have landed?'

Her initial thought was that he was joking, but when she turned to look out of the window her eyes flew wide. They really were taxiing on the runway. Her face mirrored her disappointment.

'Oh, I missed it!'

He was amused. She sounded so *young*, or maybe he just felt old today.

'There's always next time.'

'The first time is special,' she said and watched his eyes darken to velvet black. Her smile died as their eyes connected and clung.

'It should be,' he agreed, wondering if hers had been, and instinctively not liking the man who had been responsible for her first sexual experience. His own was so long ago—he really was feeling every hour of his thirty-two years at the moment—he barely remembered the event, certainly not the face of the slightly older woman who had provided his carnal initiation, he just remembered her athleticism.

The flurry of activity as the doors were opened managed to shake her free of his dark stare. Even with contact broken, the feelings low in her pelvis didn't ease.

She heard him get up and move away but didn't look up. Instead she asked herself what the hell just happened as she secured Declan securely in a baby sling, which made it easier to negotiate the steps, even with a bag containing the baby essentials banging against her hip.

Arthur was on the tarmac. He waved but walked across to Zac who had disembarked ahead of her and was speaking to someone official-looking. Even from a distance it was obvious that the official was eager to please.

Waiting to be told where to go, she stood on the tarmac, which seemed to reflect the heat it had absorbed back at her. With an anxious glance at the baby, she fished in the bag for a sunhat, which she fitted carefully on a contented Declan's head. She had anointed him with suncream during the flight, using the spare left on her own nose—even so, she could almost hear the sound of her freckles breaking out as she stood there. Despite the precautions she was anxious to get the baby out of the sun.

She delved a second time into the bag, giving a little grunt of triumph when her fingers located what she was looking for, a cheap and cheerful plastic handheld fan, which she directed at Declan.

Allowing herself a few seconds of fan use, she directed it down her cleavage before she moved it back to Declan. Her clothes were sticking to her skin as she looked around, controlling her impatience with difficulty. After the build-up of expectation she was here, and here was not very exciting. Her emotions had dipped. One stretch of tarmac was much the same as another.

She was trying to remember how long Zac had said their transfer would be when he appeared at her side.

'How long did you say it took to—'

'The helicopter transfer takes less than thirty minutes,' came the terse-sounding response. 'Before you ask, I've checked that it's OK for babies. So this helicopter will be a first for you too, I'm assuming?'

Her lips tightened. He made her sound freakish, and there was no sign of the tentative rapport of their journey. Well, if he thought it was weird that she was a first flyer imagine what he'd make of her being a virgin. Not that she'd get to know because it was not information she was about to share with him.

'There is a large part of the population, who aren't Greek billionaires, that haven't been in a helicopter.'

He didn't comment on her spiky response beyond a sardonic look that made her feel embarrassed.

'Arthur will take you to the house. I have some business I need to attend to in Athens. I'll probably stay over.'

He delivered the information as though this were the plan all along, but it wasn't a plan at all, it was more a sticking plaster. The humiliating reality was he had to put some distance between them because he couldn't think past the sexual attraction, an attraction that seemed to divest him of his normal objectivity, and turn his iron control back on itself.

Rose just nodded, wondering what the *business's* name was, and knowing that she had no right to feel a sense of hurt that lay like a boulder in her chest.

Not that she was interested. As far as she could see they all looked pretty much identical...

Wonder if he ever gets the names mixed up?

She was not at all jealous of the identikit women.

'You all right?' Arthur sounded anxious.

Rose realised that she had been staring at the back view of Zac as he strode away, seemingly unaware of heads turning to follow the tall dynamic figure.

'Fine,' she said, painting on a cheerful smile. Zac's coldness didn't hurt her at all, why would it?

'Can I carry something that isn't alive and kicking?' Arthur gave a little wave to the baby, admitting, 'I never know what to say to children.'

'Babies are pretty uncritical,' Rose, amused by the confession, assured him. If only all men found it so easy to admit to their weaknesses, life would be much simpler, she mused, thinking of one particular man. 'If you don't mind the bag...?'

She slid the bag from her aching shoulder and handed it over, smiling her gratitude. She might travel light, but a baby did not.

Zac had walked on ahead so Rose had a grandstand view of the ripple effect of his progress—like a Mexican wave, heads turned and eyes followed him.

Rose wasn't surprised. He was very watchable, though she couldn't watch him as when she reached the concourse he had vanished. She searched for a distinctive dark head above the throng but there was no sight of him.

'This way...'

Rose nodded and followed, suspicious of something like sympathy in the older man's eyes. Was he thinking *another one*...? He must have seen it before, women falling for his boss and throwing themselves at him.

Her chin lifted. Well, she wasn't one of them, she had more pride. She was there to do a job and that was what she would do, she decided, lifting a hand to shade her eyes from the sun, which was now directly overhead.

With Arthur in charge the golf-buggy transfer to the helipad was smooth. The only hitch came when they were about to lift off. The pilot, who was speaking into his mouthpiece, turned around, hand raised, and yelled above the low-level din.

CHAPTER NINE

'AN EXTRA PASSENGER, FOLKS.'

That was when Rose saw the tall figure, head bent, short hair blowing wildly in the blow back from the blades as he ran towards them. The door opened, bringing a rush of air, noise and the final passenger.

It closed and he was inside, the helicopter lifting off as he was belting in.

Rose sat there, a carefully neutral smile on her lips that gave no clue to the presence of her internal turmoil. Before she'd seen him she had been feeling positive, in control, and then he'd appeared and her little bubble of calm had burst into a million pieces.

'Change of plan.'

Rose nodded, her attitude matching his casual delivery of the sparse information, and directed her gaze out of the window.

Zac's car had actually arrived when he'd asked himself why.

Why was he reluctant to ask the question, let alone answer it? He had chosen to put distance between them because he wanted her. His response to the temptation she presented implied he didn't trust himself and Zac would not admit to this sort of weakness even to himself. Such an acknowledgment would require a redrafting of…well, his life!

At that point he sent the car away and now he was sitting looking at Rose, attacked by a desire that made every inch of his skin tingle with sexual attraction…even his scalp got in the game… It was insane but it was real.

Rose had been afraid she had such high expectations that the reality would be a bit of a let-down. When she got her first glimpse of the Villa Aphrodite she knew that wasn't going to happen.

The setting alone was worth several gasps of amazement. The sprawling terracotta-roofed building, low and built around a courtyard, had a central stone tower shaded by cypresses and pine trees. It nestled into the rock above a stretch of empty glittering sand and, beyond that, the dazzling blue ocean.

But it was as the helicopter came in to land that the scale and beauty of the building were revealed.

Part golden stone, part painted classic white, and windows facing the ocean or across lush, landscaped gardens with traditional blue frames.

It seemed to be an organic part of the landscape, not something grafted on, but blending in. She gave a series of yelps and gasps of excitement as she caught a glimpse of the pool that appeared to hang in mid-air surrounded by terraces of greenery.

'There's another one, look…'

She turned and saw Zac watching her. As if he didn't know how many swimming pools or tennis courts he had...

He watched as her almost childlike enthusiasm and spontaneous pleasure shifted into self-conscious embarrassment.

'Sorry, I...'

'Do not be sorry. I got excited when I first stumbled on this place from the air too, a wreck then, of course, but there was something about it that...' Without his being aware, his clenched hand went to his chest, pressing against the place where his heart beat as he shook his head.

The connection he obviously felt did not seem foolish to Rose. 'And you saved it?' she said, eyes sparkling. 'What a marvellous thing to do. Why was it neglected?' She could not imagine anyone not wanting to live in such a magical place.

Could there be a connection between her praise and the warm glow he was feeling? Zac dismissed the idea as absurd.

'I believe there was a family falling out that passed down through the generations, two brothers inherited, one was desperate to sell, the other refused and the place stood empty.'

'That's sad.'

It was hard to tell if she was talking about the empty home or the family dispute, but her emotions seemed genuine. She turned and caught him staring and looked self-conscious for a moment, then smiled. Her smile was genuine...she was genuine...

His promise to Marco seemed more and more like a fool's errand.

'But it had a happy ending—you brought it back to life and what a beautiful place for a child to grow up.' Her smile grew tender as it was directed at the baby who had slept all the way through the transfer. 'He really is so contented…' Her lips twitched as she saw his reaction to her claim. 'When he doesn't have colic.'

She lost her fight and the laughter she had been holding in bubbled out.

Laughter at his expense had a novelty value. There had been instances he had been tempted to spout gibberish just to see how many people congratulated him on his brilliance.

The expressions flickering across her face made him think of a time-lapse film of an opening flower bud. It was just all there. She appeared to hide nothing. She possessed a rare spontaneity.

Or maybe he was seeing what he wanted to. Was he allowing his physical attraction to cloud his judgment?

He doubted that Marco would be impressed to hear him sounding more like a cheerleader than an objective observer.

'Can you imagine growing up here?' she enthused.

Zac didn't respond. His expression was opaque but she read disapproval in his shuttered eyes. Again it was less what he said and more of what he didn't say that bothered her. Rose gave a tiny sigh, exasperated by his lightning moods that made it hard to relax around him, which was maybe, she reflected, not such a bad thing. Relax too much around him and she might be in trouble.

She didn't pursue the thought as to what the trouble might involve because the pilot had set the helicopter down smoothly on a vast area of green to one side of the house. As she peered through the window she could make out massive decorative wrought-iron gates set in a stone wall that appeared to surround the house and grounds. They stood open.

'Do you own this area outside the walls too?' Her fascination for his home overcame her determination to behave more like an employee and less like an inquisitive house guest.

This place could not have been a more dramatic contrast to his London apartment, which, with its expensive neutrality, gave very little clue to the man who occupied it, other than the fact he had limitless resources, but there was none of *him* in the place, or so it seemed to Rose. But then maybe that was him, slick, and expensive?

He glanced her way before nodding and shading his eyes as he followed the direction of her gaze.

'The land goes all the way to the public road, about a mile away, and then the lower slopes of the mountain.' He nodded to the steep, densely wooded hillside.

'That is a *biggish* garden,' she said, eyes wide. 'So this is an estate?'

He shrugged casually but didn't dispute her description. 'Many hectares are forested but we have some productive olives. The family who owned it sold off sections of land over the years. I negotiated to buy some back—it is a work in progress.'

'You make your own olive oil?' She was charmed by the idea.

He laughed. 'There is a little too much for just domestic use. We supply a few outlets around the world. Artisan products have a big market these days.' He watched her looking impatiently through the window, her childlike impatience amusing him—until it annoyed him. 'They'll have finished offloading the luggage in a moment.'

'I bet you have some lovely family parties here.' She watched the shutters come down, which should have told her to back off but it only made her more curious.

'I believe they do.' Though his family had considered him mad when he took on the task of the renovation, they were all happy enough now to spend holidays here frequently en masse.

'They?' she wondered out loud, a frown tugging at her smooth brow.

'I am a busy man. Besides,' he threw over his shoulder as he rose, 'a GGW might eat the guests.' He watched the mortified heat climb into her cheeks, and felt a scratch of guilt, but his jibe had effectively diverted her from her line of questioning.

'You heard…?'

His grin was very white. 'I appreciated the gorgeous.'

'Like you didn't know,' she muttered under her

breath, her discomfort mingled with indignation because he seemed to be enjoying her embarrassment.

'Like you didn't know, Mr Adamos,' he corrected with mocking solemnity.

Arthur's arrival denied her the right of reply, which was not a bad thing because you couldn't really call your boss the things she wanted to—even if he was one!

On terra firma, Rose was immediately conscious that the air smelt different. She inhaled a few lungsful of the fragrance that the aerial view had not revealed.

'Thyme, mint, rosemary,' he said, watching her. 'They all grow wild here with a strong hint of cypress and sea salt. If you could bottle it you'd make a fortune.'

'It's beautiful,' she said, glancing across as someone slammed a Jeep door.

'The luggage,' he explained. 'There's room for you if you want a ride.'

'I'll walk, thanks.' She wanted to take it all in. 'I've been sitting down all day. I need to stretch my legs.'

He glanced down. She was wearing the baby, who was awake and looking happy against her breasts— who wouldn't?—in the sling arrangement. 'It's a bit of a hill.' He took a deep breath. 'I'll take him.'

She swung around, the surprise in her eyes melting into approval, which he wasn't looking for, although it made sense for him to get used to the baby.

'Great. The sling is quite easy really. It'll need adjusting. You're not my size but—'

'No,' Zac interrupted the flow. There were limitations, and wearing the baby carrier was one of them. 'I'll carry him, if you trust me.'

'Of course!' she said, sounding outraged at the idea she wouldn't as she freed the baby from the baby carrier and carefully transferred him to Zac. 'You're his...' She paused. 'Are you going to adopt him?'

'Apparently that is an option. Liam will always be Declan's father.'

'Of course, but a boy needs a dad too. Your father died but he is still your father.'

Zac pulled himself back from the edge of throwing the truth back at her, revealing that, as much as he'd like to forget his father, he never could. That he'd spent his life watching for signs that he was anything like the dead man, guarding against anything resembling a paternal character trait that was hiding in his DNA, that he needed control to do that and now she was in danger of splintering it... She was pounding away at the protective wall he'd built in a way that no one had before.

He even kept his family that side of the protective wall built to shield the people he cared for, not himself.

The thoughts slid through his head, invisible behind the cold mask he wore. 'I am aware of that.'

She had hit a nerve. How, why, she had no idea.

Zac seemed deep in thought. His body language did not encourage conversation as they walked up the hill, which actually was quite steep. Breathless by the time she reached the top, she was glad he was carrying the baby.

They walked through the open gates into a cobbled courtyard filled with a succession of bubbling fountains and geometric flower beds spilling colour onto the stone. The sea, which had been to their left as they climbed the hill, was now directly in front of them, visible above the terracotta-tiled roof where the aquamarine blended seamlessly into the blue of the sky, but revealed more dramatically through a massive stone arch that acted as a portrait frame for a breathtaking view of the gardens running down to the sand and endless sea.

Enchanted, she spread her arms wide as though embracing the view. 'How do you ever leave here?' she wondered out loud.

Zac normally felt a lightening of his mood as he stepped through the gates, but on this occasion the magic failed to work. The weight that had lain across his shoulders, a burden that was not physical, did not lift as he walked into the courtyard.

But as Rose spoke and he heard the unfiltered pleasure in her voice and read the uncomplicated joy on her face he felt lighter.

Her unfeigned pleasure was contagious. She was living totally in the moment, which was a rare ability.

'I had no idea…' She looked from right to left, saw the whitewashed walls glinting in the sun, taking in the sheer size of the place. 'It's so big! Did you extend on the original building?'

'It was hard to tell how big the place was originally. It was derelict and there were no records and the locals seem to think that the villa I rebuilt was built on the site of a previous villa that was much grander. The old landscaped gardens, which we uncovered by accident, could have belonged to that earlier building. They were certainly very elaborate for what was an olive farm.'

'You recreated the gardens.' What she had seen of them was impressive.

'As much as possible, we kept what original features in the house there were and used reclaimed materials in the build for the most part. There are some skilled craftsmen locally. They were ingenious in recreating incomplete and damaged features.'

Rose nodded. She couldn't wait to see the interior.

'Come,' he added, glancing at her hair that blazed in the sunlight as he gestured to the building they stood in front of. 'I think we could do with some shade.'

Rose gave a self-recriminatory grimace and glanced anxiously at Declan. She had been so busy admiring the building that she had neglected her charge.

'Sorry,' she said, following him through the arch. He paused, looking mystified. 'Why?'

'I was chattering on while the baby…his skin needs protecting.'

'The baby has barely a centimetre of skin exposed. It was your skin I was thinking about.' Almost continually. The thought of feasting his eyes on the smooth paleness, of exploring it with his fingers, tongue and mouth, feeling her skin cool or hot beneath him…had become a constant. And now the images, sparked into life by his thoughts, glutted his senses, requiring a long sense-cooling moment before he could continue speaking without betraying himself and his growing obsession.

'You are very fair. Redheads burn, don't they? You should wear a hat while you're here.'

'Yes, I suppose I should… I freckle terribly.' She touched her small straight nose and grimaced.

'I like freckles.'

Rose told herself not to be flattered. There was liking and *liking* and it was telling that the assets his dates boasted were not freckles!

Without warning he walked away. Rose started to follow, glancing around curiously as she hurried to keep him in sight. There was a lot to take in. The infinity pool below a terrace that surrounded this side of the villa took second place to the blue blaze of the shimmering sea beyond. The building itself was on three sides of where they stood. There were several arches cut into the stone smaller than the one they had entered, but beyond she had glimpses of what seemed to be a series of internal courtyards.

He led her to a doorway, not as large as the one in the outer courtyard, and swung around without warning, causing her to step back and the baby to gurgle excitedly.

CHAPTER TEN

'I LIKE YOUR stutter too.' The words emerged almost sounding as if he had spoken against his will.

Rose's mind froze at the unexpected compliment and the air of compulsion with which he delivered it.

Was there a punchline?

Was he joking?

His expression didn't suggest anything so harmless and light-hearted, but neither was there anything remotely seductive in his clenched mouth and taut, almost angry stare.

Kick-starting her brain, she followed him into the interior, finding herself standing in what seemed to be an inner hallway filled with scent from the massive terracotta bowl of rosemary in flower, the pale pastel purple of the flowers pale against the deep green of the leaves.

There were several doors leading off it, but she struggled to keep up with his low-voiced explanation or the decoration, maybe both. She simply couldn't focus so she gave up trying as he spoke about the massive arched, bleached supportive beam overhead being reclaimed from an ancient tree on the estate that had come down in a storm.

All she could think was…he *likes* my stutter.

It took her a few moments to connect the buzz of silence with the fact he was no longer speaking, which meant that she ought to be. 'It is very beautiful.'

It was. The floor underfoot was some sort of limed wood, the beams of the high ceiling exposed the dark rafters that provided a dramatic foil for rough whitewashed stone, the few items of furniture were all rustic and the original artwork on the walls provided dramatic splashes of colour.

'But do you get the general layout?' He sounded impatient. 'It's quite simple if you just keep in mind that—'

'Yes,' she lied without hesitation. No way would she admit she hadn't heard a word he had said.

'So, Camille will see you to your rooms, show you the nursery facilities and, when you are ready, sit with Declan while you have dinner.'

For the first time she noticed the slim dark haired girl who was standing just behind her. 'Thank you, Camille,' she said, smiling at the girl. 'But it will be easier if I have dinner in my room. I don't like to leave Declan.'

'Camille, as I have explained, is perfectly capable of looking after a baby. We are lucky to have her to help out during the university vacation.'

The dark-haired young woman looked pleased at the compliment, and, being a female with a brain and not an overactive imagination, *she* didn't over-react and think his comment had any deep hidden message.

'I like babies when I can hand them back.'

Her English was faultless.

'As I said, Camille has six younger siblings so plenty of experience and she will be available to help out most days. Oh, and do not say bad things about the housekeeper in front of her—she is Sybil's niece.' He added a postscript in Greek, which made the brunette laugh.

'Oh, well, yes, that would be…fine, then, I think…?' Given the option of protesting further would make her look slightly unhinged, she put as good a face on the situation as possible. There was always the chance that she would be dining alone…

'Can I take him?' the young girl asked, flashing Rose a questioning look as she walked towards Zac.

Rose felt a wave of relief. It wasn't as if she'd been *dreading* stepping in close to take Declan off his guardian, but to be relieved of that moment was not something she was going to refuse.

She watched the transfer from a safe distance, if a safe distance existed when it came to Zac and his overwhelming masculinity.

She watched as his arrogant profile softened, the lines radiating from the corners of his eyes deepening as he smiled down at the baby, and Rose felt as if a hand had reached inside her chest and squeezed hard.

Common sense told her this was about hormones,

and primitive urges. She wasn't going to pretend these things were not happening, but she didn't have to over-analyse them. It didn't matter how or why this was happening now, it was, and she just had to deal with it.

There was no point being defeatist. She couldn't allow this…hormone thing to ruin what could be a fantastic experience. It was pathetic, so passive.

If she was to enjoy the opportunity to appreciate her Greece stay, she needed a coping strategy. She'd tried to pretend it wasn't happening and that hadn't worked. So a new strategy, and for starters she wasn't going to over-analyse it.

Because maybe you wouldn't like the answers?

She knew a nettle would bring her out in a rash, so she didn't touch it. It made sense not to touch Zac. Could it be that simple?

She sighed. If only… A nettle didn't have a voice that stroked the nerve endings in her skin like a caress, it didn't have a mouth… Actually the entire analogy was rubbish, whichever way you looked at it.

'Hello, baby… Oh, he's so lovely… Come on, baby Declan, let's show you your room.'

Rose waited until she saw which door the young woman was headed for then followed. She didn't look but she knew his eyes were following her, the skin on the nape of her neck tingling, the tiny hairs on her skin dancing.

The nursery suite, when they reached it, was charming. And, considering it must literally have been created overnight, remarkably well equipped—from the drawers of neatly folded baby clothes to the colourful playroom filled with toys.

It had its own little kitchen complete with some chilled wine in the fridge, which she assumed was a thoughtful addition for her, though she had to question the professionalism of sampling it in charge of a baby. She left Camille while she did a quick tour of her own section of the suite.

Her bedroom, utterly charming with a cool dark wooden floor and bleached oak furniture, was a million miles from anything she had ever lived with. No flatpack cheap and cheerful, but items with workmanship that spoke of hours and hours of the loving care and skill that went into each individual piece's creation. She walked through the open French door onto a Juliet balcony that looked directly onto the infinity pool she had spotted from the air, and the sea beyond.

If the bedroom was charming, her bathroom was genuine *wow*! The stone-lined shower had high-tech digital controls that were slightly daunting. What was tempting and not daunting was the free-standing copper bath deep enough to float in that was set beside a full-height window that overlooked the ocean.

Rose could easily imagine herself setting up residence in the bath—with that view, what would be the reason to get out? Longing to linger and maybe try out the decadent tub, she hurried back to the nursery kitchen where Camille was humming a soft melody to a heavy-eyed Declan.

She smiled and lifted a finger to her lips when she saw Rose. 'I changed him,' she whispered, adding a mouthed, Shall I put him in his crib…?

Rose nodded and felt slightly redundant. Camille seemed super-efficient. She left her to it and followed the coffee smell and poured herself a cup, then, putting her bottom onto one of the high stools that faced a small island unit, sat and waited for Camille.

She didn't have long to wait. 'He was asleep before I put him down.'

'Thanks,' Rose said, lifting her mug, and added, 'This too. Just what I was longing for.'

'No need to thank me. If I wasn't here I'd be babysitting my twin brothers who are eleven, so thank you, you have saved me!'

'What university do you go to?'

'Athens. I'm in my final year, maths, but I just got accepted at Imperial for my masters, so this job is useful. Actually I wouldn't be going at all if it wasn't for Mr Adamos.'

'How so?'

'Well, not him personally, at least that's what he said when I thanked him, but the Adamos Foundation provides bursaries for students who have brains but no cash—that's me,' she said cheerily.

'That's fantastic. When you come to London you'll have to look me up.'

'You live in London? I'm so jealous.'

'You live here. I'm so jealous!'

They both laughed.

When Camille left it was agreed that she'd return to babysit around seven-thirty when she said dinner was served.

She actually arrived at six-thirty with a laptop and a stack of books. Rose was still in a big fluffy robe from a hamper with a pile of them in the bathroom. Her hair, half dried, hung loose and almost to her waist.

'I'm late!' she exclaimed when Camille appeared.

'No, I'm early. I'm always early,' the girl admitted. 'Can I do anything?'

'No, Declan has had his bath and feed and he's settled well. Apparently he had colic quite badly recently, so if you have any problems you will come and get me...'

'Of course, no problem, go eat, but maybe get dressed first?'

Rose laughed and whisked away to her bedroom. Picking an outfit was quite simple as there was a choice of two and the cotton sundress was creased even after she had hung it in the bathroom in the hope of getting the creases out. She was sure that she could have just asked and an iron would have appeared but the second option was fine.

The pair of wide-legged trousers had folded to almost nothing in her bag but as she laid them on the bed the silky black fabric was totally crease-free. She had brought a couple of white tee shirts to team with them in the daytime but the black boxy-shaped top, sleeveless with a simple scoop neck in the front and a deep vee in the back, was her go-to for more dressy occasions.

Under her gown she was wearing a tiny silky bra and pants. After she pulled the trousers up over her hips and fastened the zip she realised that she must have lost a few pounds since she'd last worn them, but the cut covered a multitude of sins except, in this instance, her waist. She hitched them higher but they slid down again. Even if she'd had a belt to secure them, there were no belt loops.

No point stressing, it wasn't noticeable and the top would disguise the problem—except of course it didn't. The boxy-cut top ended where the waistband of the trousers began, which was perfect but became less than perfect when she moved. Every time she did a sliver of stomach came into view, not exactly illegal or even particularly daring but tonight it made her uneasy.

Not a lot to do about that, she decided, except maybe not move… Finding the block-heeled mules she'd brought, she slipped them on, raising her height by three inches. She bent towards the mirror, to check out the make-up she had applied earlier. She had to lean in a little closer because there wasn't much of it. After a moment's reflection she added a swipe of mascara to her already dark lashes and a smudge of grey eyeshadow, and applied a second coat of gloss to her lips.

There was no time to tame her hair, so she bent forward and ran her fingers through the auburn strands before tossing it back with a drastic swoosh. She didn't want to look as if she was trying too hard, or at all really.

Looking at her reflection in the mirror, Rose laughed and thought, Not much chance of that! And trying too hard for whom? The chances were she would be eating alone and she was acting as though she were on a date! And she was getting all stomach fluttery on the off chance he'd join her.

But he hadn't said he *wouldn't* be joining her.

She looked in on the sleeping baby, his face illuminated by the night light on a dresser. The impulse to pick him up and hold him, and most likely wake him up, was hard to resist. Her smile faded as she thought of generations of nannies who cared for children, loved them and in some cases were the only parent the child knew, only to be given their marching orders when the child got too old to need a nanny.

Heartbreaking… She had only been caring for Declan for a couple of days but already she knew that it would be desperately hard to say goodbye. How soon did it take to fall in love? It was love at first sight for many mothers, and some adoptive parents too who hadn't given birth… It was as if the helplessness of a baby roused protective impulses, brought out the nurturing instincts.

Quietly leaving the room, she looked in on Camille, who was perched on one of the high stools in the kitchen, her computer and books set up on the work surface.

'Wow, you look great!' she said when she saw Rose.

Rose smiled. 'Thanks. You know where I am if you need me,' she said, which was more than she did.

As if reading her thoughts Camille ripped a page from her notepad. 'Though this might help until you get your bearings.'

Rose took the paper and studied a detailed neat line plan of the villa.

'You will note the *"we are here"* and bingo is where you're going.'

'Oh, that is just so kind. I have the worst sense of direction,' she admitted ruefully. 'I spent half an hour trying to find a particular department store in a shopping precinct and then an hour trying to find the exit. I was too embarrassed to ask for help.'

The girl chuckled. 'See you later and don't worry about the time. I've got plenty to keep me occupied.'

Rose tried to pick out landmarks to help her remember the route as she navigated her way using the plan. When she arrived at the bingo door it was half open. She folded the plan and tucked it in the pocket of her trousers, and, taking a deep breath, she tapped on the door, called out, 'Hello,' and walked inside.

The room was empty. She told herself she was glad as her eyes moved around the room, taking in the open doors and the terrace beyond. The dark table was set for two, candles as yet unlit, and she hoped they stayed that way, in an eclectic selection of rustic holders, different sizes and textures, some glass, some wood, beautiful and also disturbingly intimate.

Her eyes centred on the wine chilling in the bucket of ice. Dutch courage or not, it was a good thing that the cork was undisturbed or she might have been tempted, because as appealing as the thought of a glass was, she was in charge of a baby.

As she walked around the room taking in all the quirky artistic touches, it was hard to believe that the man who lived here was the same man who based himself in the soulless London flat.

The answer to the mystery was probably as simple as two different interior designers.

A noise behind her made her spin around, heart pumping. When she saw Arthur standing in the doorway the anticlimax was intense. *All pumped up and nowhere to go*, mocked the voice in her head.

'Hi there,' he said, hovering half in and half out of the room.

She painted on a bright smile. 'Are we eating together?'

He looked initially startled by the suggestion, then laughed. 'What? Oh, no, the boss sent me to apologise, he's stuck on a call. He said for you to start without him.'

'I wasn't sure he was joining me…' But the possibility had filled her stomach with butterflies…and made her add the mascara. She glanced at the empty table. 'Start what?'

'God, yes, sorry.' He entered the room and walked over to a slate-topped table, pressed a button and doors glided apart revealing shelves housing containers… quite obviously food, by the smell.

'The boss had this contraption made to order. He works some pretty unsocial hours, and eats the same way, actually sometimes forgets to eat. This saves the staff hanging around waiting. He thought you might appreciate the informality, first night and all, long journey…'

Rose received this information in silence.

Arthur was looking at her a little uncertainly, as if he was struggling to gauge her reaction. 'You tuck in.'

'Oh, I will,' she promised, floating out a brilliant and brittle smile.

When he had gone she stood there and swore. Well, she'd got what she wanted: a nice peaceful dinner with no Zac Adamos making her feel self-conscious and ill at ease. Yet at the same time there was a connection that she couldn't explain. It was as if looking at him she were looking into a mirror and seeing the things about herself she kept secret from the world…even herself…

The idea made her feel uneasy as she walked over and began to lift lids. From chilled soup to chicken in some sort of delicate sauce that smelt wonderful, it all looked delicious. She unenthusiastically ladled some soup into a dish and carried it to the table. She had lost her appetite, and her wandering glance landed on the chilling bottle.

She stood up and reached across, pulling it from the ice with a smile of defiance on her lips. Pulling the cork was less easy than she had anticipated. She struggled with it for a minute or so but when it came she got the dramatic flourish she'd wanted. It exploded like...well, like a bottle of champagne that someone had just shaken half to death.

The white tablecloth had absorbed most of the liquid but there were some small pools on the polished wood floor. She looked in the bottle and laughed as her anger drained away, leaving her feeling pretty foolish and very glad there had been no one around to witness her temper tantrum, and all that breathless anticipation that she had refused to recognise for what it was—a passing meaningless comment. With a groan she lifted the bottle to her lips and drained the last teaspoon of champagne that remained in the bottle.

Just because he said he liked my stutter! Rose closed her eyes, feeling unbelievably stupid.

CHAPTER ELEVEN

BACK IN THE NURSERY, Camille was surprised to see her so soon.

'I wasn't very hungry.'

The girl wrinkled her nose. 'What is that smell?'

'I had an incident with a glass of wine.' She tugged at her top, which was clinging unpleasantly.

'Oh, that's… She looked at Rose's face. 'So not a good evening?'

'Not so much,' Rose agreed.

'Do you want me to do anything? There's coffee on the go.'

Rose smiled her gratitude. 'No, you get off and I'll get out of these soggy things. How was Declan?'

'Great. He woke after you'd left but once I patted his back for a while he went straight back off.'

When Camille had collected her things and left Rose headed for her room, desperate to strip off and shower. She paused in the doorway of the nursery, smiling as she heard the sound of his even breathing.

She walked over to the cot and looked down at the baby-soft features, and wondered how her own mother could have walked away from her. If you couldn't trust your own mother, who could you trust? Which was one reason she was never going to put her trust in another person. If that meant she became a sad woman with a cat, so what? It was better than being rejected.

'They wouldn't have left you, never think that. Your mum and dad would have loved you. Your new dad will love you too.'

A child should always know they were loved and wanted.

Rose had reached her bedroom when she heard a soft tap on the door. Assuming that Camille had forgotten something, she swallowed her irritation and went to answer it.

She opened the door and her glance travelled upwards, stopping when it reached his face. The sensual jolt to her senses when she saw him standing there had stalled her brain, cognitive thought was not on the agenda, just shaking and feeling, feeling too much. It was a definite overload.

Zac's nostrils flared at the odour of alcohol. Realising his suspicion was correct gave him no satisfaction.

He was angry, but also felt pity, though it was hard to feel sympathy for someone who was throwing away their life. He'd known people who'd lost everything…but some came back after reaching rock bottom.

'Is Camille here?'

Rose shook her head, not trusting her vocal cords to respond.

'Then I think I'd better come in,' he said grimly.

Her chin went up. 'And I think you'd better not,' she retorted.

'Look, it's none of my business what you do to yourself but when you're in charge of a baby that is very much my business.'

She planted her hands on her hips, angling a look of angry mystification up at him. 'What the hell are you t-talking about?'

'There's no point denying it, you reek of the stuff.'

'Reek of…?' The dots in her head suddenly connected and made crazy sense. 'You think I've been drinking?'

Her voice was so low he could barely catch the words. At least she wasn't slurring, not yet anyhow. How was he going to tell Marco? *Was* he going to tell Marco?

Where the hell did that crazy thought come from? Enabling an addict was not protecting them… Protecting. Why had that been his first instinct and since when did protecting a woman he'd known for five minutes trump the loyalty to one of his oldest friends?

'Look, there are people that can help. The first thing you have to do is accept you have a problem.'

Her eyes narrowed. 'Oh, I know I have a problem and it's six feet four and a half,' she sneered, allowing her eyes to run the head-to-toe length of his long, lean body. 'You think I'd get drunk when I'm looking after a baby! You're the one who left wine in the fridge. What do you think I am? Cancel that,' she added bitterly. 'I already know. Oh, God, I think I hate you!'

Zac's nostrils flared as he fought to contain his anger. 'Don't try and turn this around. I saw the empty bottle. I smelt the booze.'

'Of course you smelt the booze, you stupid man! The bloody bottle exploded when I tried to open it. It went everywhere. I took a champagne shower!' An expression of distaste on her face, she plucked at her wet clinging top.

'You…?' For the first time he took in her damp trousers and drenched top that lovingly outlined the hard peaks of her taut breasts. His head went back as he half smiled and gave a sigh of relief.

'How could you think I would do that? If you don't believe me, breathalyse me.'

'I don't have one on me at the moment.'

'Right, then, smell…' Grabbing his jacket, she stretched up until her forehead was level with his chin. His head bent, and a thrill of excitement shot through her as their glances connected and held.

What are you doing, Rose?

She reacted to the sliver of sanity by sinking down onto her heels and releasing his jacket, only to find her efforts countered by a strong arm that had snaked around her waist. Instead of sinking down she found her toes trailing on the ground and her upper body crushed against a chest that had no give.

'I…'

A finger hooked under her chin refused to allow her to escape his burning, stomach-melting stare.

'It's hard to tell from smell alone.'

'Well, you'll just have to t-trust me,' she responded shakily, barely able to hear her whisper above the sound of her laboured rasping inhalations.

'How about tasting you? I remember how you tasted.'

The throaty purr sent a fresh rush of debilitating weakness through her body. Her knees sagged and her clamped lips couldn't stop a lost cry of longing escaping, and then there was no escape. Her breath was mingled with his as his tongue slid into her mouth. She focused on the taste of him as their tongues collided, starting a primal chain reaction that swept her away... She gasped, feeling his hand on her breast, causing him to pull back enough to bite her lip and stare with burning eyes into her passion-flushed face.

'Do you believe I'm sober now?' she rasped, not recognising her own voice, or the deep desire to feel all of the power of his hard body, to feel him unleashed... Shiver after shiver of excitement ran through her body. For the first time in her ordered adult life, she longed to let go, to lose control.

But this was not right, this was too soon, he was not her soulmate, he was not the special someone she could trust with her life or her heart... The tipping point came when she looked up at him and knew that she wanted him more than she wanted to stay safe in her emotionally sterile bubble.

'That strip and shower… I like that idea…'

She gave a tiny mute affirmative nod of her head.

'You know I want you,' he rasped sealing their bodies thigh to thigh.

She swallowed. 'It feels that way.'

'Your skin tastes of champagne…nice…' he murmured, running his tongue along the curve of her jaw. 'But I'd prefer it tasted of me. That *I* tasted of you.'

'Oh, God!' She groaned against his mouth, the dark dirty images his words evoked making her weak with lust. 'Yes, please.'

She felt so light when he picked her up, her bones so delicate, her skin so soft, she was so fragile… But the small hands that slid down his back massaging the muscles had strength and determination he quite definitely approved of as she began to slip the buttons on his shirt, sliding her flat palm over the now damp skin of his chest and shoulders.

It was a short distance to the decadent bathroom but they were both panting like runners approaching the finishing post when he placed her on her feet. For a second her gaze was drawn past him as Rose caught sight of herself in a mirror. The person who stared back at her was a stranger. She barely recognised herself, the hectic flush of arousal on her cheeks, the incandescent glow in her eyes… She not only felt like a different person, she looked like one too.

'You're shaking.'

She nodded mutely.

The tremors that shook her began deep in her core, the waves spreading out involving every nerve ending, every inch of her skin.

He framed her face in his hands and drew back slightly. 'You're burning up.'

She was burning for him.

She nodded and sealed her fate. The need that consumed him beyond logical explanation was greater than his loyalty to a friend, greater than any other consideration at that moment.

'Then you don't need this.'

Zac held her eyes as he took the hem of her top. Not trying to escape his carnal stare, she felt more aroused than she had ever imagined possible. Rose lifted her arms and he peeled the sodden, spoiled garment over her head and dropped it on the floor.

Rose reached for her bra and unfastened the clip, letting her breasts spring free as it fell to the floor. She lifted her chin. She didn't have a clue why she wasn't self-conscious. It was as if he had awakened something in her that had lain dormant. She had never felt sexy and desirable before in this way— the idea of a man like Zac wanting her was incredibly arousing.

His eyes darkened as he stared down at the hard-peaked soft mounds. 'Perfect.' He kissed her hard on the lips before weighing one smooth rosy-tipped globe in the palm of his hand. She whimpered as he rubbed his thumb across the peak, drawing a series of low moans from her lips, before he replaced it with his lips and tongue.

She clung so hard to stop falling down that his shirt was half undone by the time his ministrations stopped. Her eyes flew wide as he dropped to his knees, then, with one hand spanning her narrow rib-cage, he used his free hand to unzip her trousers and slide them down her thighs.

She was giving him the power to hurt her, and she had never imagined feeling this way, accepting the possibility was there but willing to take the risk. Maybe one day she would regret this decision but now, in this moment, she knew if she didn't take the leap into the unknown there was no question she *would* regret never knowing.

She shivered even though the wildness in her veins, the heat rising up in her, were like a furnace. He began to strip and she forgot how to breathe. He was ripping his clothes off in a frenzy of impatience, an impatience that she shared. She wanted passion to burn away all the doubts and fears that had been there all her life. She wanted to lose herself in him.

His chest was bare and he had just kicked away his trousers, naked but for the boxers that hung low on his narrow hips, inadequate to hide the strength of his arousal.

'I need...' She stopped, rose up on her toes and curved her hands around the back of Zac's head, her fingers sliding into his thick hair, her aching breasts pressed against his hair-roughened chest. Her hands slid over the smooth satiny muscles defining his shoulders, then lower to his waist.

As they kissed hungrily, teeth clashing, tongues

tangling and probing, she was so focused that she didn't register the fact his hands had slid under her bottom and he had picked her up until he stepped with her into the shower enclosure and switched on the water.

The shock of the warm water pummelling her skin made her gasp as he put her on her feet, and she stood, her head back, as he dragged the pants down her legs. A second later he performed the same task for himself.

The wet, slick skin-to-skin contact drew a keening cry of pleasure from Rose's throat. She felt soft and small, feminine compared to Zac's hard masculinity. The abrasive pressure of his erection against her belly sent the ache between her legs to another level. She rubbed herself against him, the friction feeding the consuming hunger that was exploding inside her, and let his eyes devour her.

She enjoyed this wanton version of herself, she even enjoyed being shocked by it. It was wildly liberating.

His molten eyes glowed. He looked fierce and dangerous, his hair and body slicked with water as he smiled a slow wicked smile, and she felt as if her heart would stop.

She saw the soap in his hands and had no idea how it had got there. She leaned against the wall, head tilted back, an expression of rapt enjoyment on her face as the water pummelled.

He soaped her breasts, his hands massaging and stroking, driving her wild, paying special attention to her painfully erect nipples before sliding his hands lower and then dropping on his knees. The stubble on his cheek and jaw burned her inner thigh. She was floating in a mindless, sensual haze of need that infiltrated every cell of her body.

'What…?' Her eyes flew wide with protest and then he was back, a foil packet in his hand. 'I'll keep you safe, don't worry.'

She knew what he meant but there was another sort of safe—a safe he would never give her—

She closed off the line of thought before it took her into forbidden territory—if she had regrets it would not be now.

Holding her gaze, he took her hands and pressed them to the wall of the cubicle, walking into her until their bodies collided slick skin against slick skin.

If there ever had been a moment to tell him that this was her first time it wasn't now. The possibility that he might walk away, leaving her quite broken, was not a risk she could take.

His hands cupped her buttocks. As he lifted her up his gaze was searing. 'Wrap your legs around me and hold on.'

Her head fell onto his shoulder as she did as he asked, her slim legs tight around his waist. She moaned at the hard male contact, the pressure at the apex of her legs as her sex throbbed with a need that matched his, and she moved suggestively against him following instincts as old as time, making no secret of the fact she wanted him.

An animal groan broke from the vault of his chest

as Zac slid into her heat, gasping at the tightness of her as she closed around him.

Her back arched, her head falling back to expose the beautiful arc of her neck, the line between pleasure and pain blurred, and she felt a moment's panic. What if she did it wrong?

'Don't know what to…' Her voice cracked and she bit into his shoulder.

The truth came to him and the shock that reverberated through him gave way to a possessive tenderness that he had never experienced before. He had never slept with a virgin before, never felt the primal urge to be any woman's first lover.

'Relax…there are no rules except the ones we make.'

'This is…you are incredible!' She gasped, feeling the tingle of her blood as she moved to meet him, draw him deeper, his throaty voice in her ear saying words she didn't need translating, his breath on her skin. She could feel the beautiful sleek, hard muscle of him everywhere. Her nerve endings were screaming a tactile blending with the pounding thud of her tumultuous pulse. The paper-thin skin of her delicate eyelids was no protection from his hot dark gaze as he pushed her towards a goal just out of reach—then it wasn't out of reach. The breath-catching crescendo, when it hit her, was so intense she clung to him, afraid of being washed away by the tsunami of sensation as his sleek, muscular body surged powerfully against hers.

In the final moment of perfect fusion Rose called

out his name in the last shuddering surge as the ec-
stasy hit.

She felt as though she were floating but in reality
she was sinking to the floor of the shower. Their eyes
sealed, they knelt, arms wrapped around each other
as they fought for breath.

'Oh, God!' she said finally. 'That was…oh, God!'
She wanted to laugh and cry. Instead she pushed her
face into his shoulder.

'That was good sex.'

She felt tension slide into her shoulders. Was the
emphasis she heard on *sex* real or imagined, and
was the silent *just* she heard the addition of her own
paranoia?

Rose wished it were. It was a mystery how one
person could make love and the other could just have
sex—

She stopped herself taking this depressing thought
to the next level. She was going to get her heart broken, that was a given, but why anticipate the moment? It made much more sense to enjoy the moment
that they were living.

As she disentangled herself from him and at-
tempted to stand up, her legs folded. They were
shaking, a reaction to the intensity of what they had
shared.

'Are you all right?' He was on his own feet in a
split second, a hand stretched out to pull her up, the
other behind him to turn the water off.

She accepted it, crossing her free hand across
her breasts, the display of modesty definitely a

'closing the stable door after the horse has already bolted' gesture.

'What can I say? You make me go weak at the knees.' Sometimes the truth was the best defence but not this time—she missed jokey by a country mile. It was the moment to stop digging or in this case talking…only she couldn't. 'I've never made—had sex in a shower before.' On the plus side, she closed her mouth before she could ask him if he had shower sex often.

'I am aware of that,' he responded in a voice loaded with meaning. 'A little warning upfront might have been good, do you not think?'

So he knew.

She wasn't sure how to deal with the unspoken question so she ignored it. Maybe he was actually quite glad she had dodged the issue, because though she thought he might press her, instead his glance slid from hers. Perhaps he wasn't so comfortable with discussing it either.

'Thanks,' she murmured as he draped a large bath sheet around her. There was nothing lover-like about the gesture but it felt almost more intimate than sex. His gentleness brought a lump to her throat. She had stripped naked and not felt a scrap of self-consciousness yet having him gently pat her dry overwhelmed her with shyness. That was, she acknowledged, deeply strange.

While he covered her Zac didn't seem in any hurry to cover himself. He had a total lack of inhibitions, which was a situation she could live with.

He really was beautiful, she reflected, following him with her eyes as he padded across to one of the heated ladder rails and grabbed a towel, which he looped casually around his middle, pausing to rub his forearm across the misted mirror.

She gave a helpless sigh of appreciation—every etched and carved line of his sleek muscled body was perfection. But mid appreciation she was hit by a sudden avalanche of emotions, intertwined and confusing. She had to stop thinking about it. She needed to follow his prompt and adopt Zac's attitude. It was sex, great sex, but just sex.

Except of course it wasn't, not for her. The emotions involved had been intense, scarily so. She pushed it all away, suddenly too tired to think about it. This was the new Rose who lived in the moment and extracted every last drop of living from it.

She was in her bathroom with a naked man.

What happened next?

'What happens next is we take this to the bedroom.'

Rose clamped a hand to her mouth—she'd said it out loud.

'If that is something you would like?'

'That would be nice.' *Nice, Rose! Really...?*

'Yes, I think it would be very nice too.' The fact was he could not get enough of her. She took the hand he stretched out and he pulled her towards him before scooping her up and carrying her into the bedroom, the feel of her warm, damp, soft body reawakening his hunger.

* * *

Zac knew he'd crossed a line Marco-wise but, given the same choice, he'd have done the same thing again. It was a line he'd been aching to cross since the first second he saw her. Nothing to do with logic—it was on an instinctive level.

He'd known it would be incredible…and *Theos*! It had surpassed anything he had imagined, but to realise that she had come to him a virgin! The revelation ought to have horrified him but instead it had just fed the possessiveness that she brought out in him.

He had built his life with walls of isolation that afforded him, and more importantly those he cared for, safety. For the first time those walls had taken a battering. In a matter of hours Rose Hill had done some serious damage. She'd made him think what it would be like to bring her inside his walls and keep her safe that way.

Rose's level of anticipation was off the scale as he laid her down on the bed and joined her, leaning over her, one hand braced on the headboard, the other caressing her face.

'I thought you didn't date staff.'

Zac barely heard her. He was seeing her soft lips open to him and thinking of her legs opening to him.

He kissed her as if he'd drain her before saying thickly, 'I don't. But you are not staff, you are…Rose.'

'I'm special.' She bit her lips and stopped herself adding 'not just convenient'. She didn't want to know, she just wanted this.

She just wanted him.

'I want you so much I'm sick with it,' he husked, trailing kisses up her neck until he found her mouth before pulling the billowing sheet over them and burrowing into her softness.

'This is…' He had reached midway down her belly and she had forgotten how to breathe.

His head lifted, the bands of colour along his cheekbone highlighting the razor edges. His eyes were dark and hot enough to drown in.

'You don't like it?

'I love it… I love…' She paused, her eyes squeezed tight as she said the forbidden words in her head… *I love you.* 'All of it,' she added out loud. She felt the heat of his mouth on her again and squeezed her eyes tight. 'And I like everything you do,' she declared with admirable understatement.

He encouraged her insatiable curiosity for exploring his body until it came to the point when her lips and tongue were eating into his self-control.

He took her hands, pinned them above her head and kissed her, not hard but with a debilitating tenderness that brought tears of emotion to her eyes.

'Have you any idea how many fantasies about your body I have had?'

Her breath came quick and fast, the tingle under her skin now a fire.

'Let's try slow, shall we, and see how that works out?'

Afraid to break the spell his voice had woven, she said nothing as he touched her face, one brown finger tracing a path down her jaw then across the fullness of her plump lower lip. Rose opened her mouth and caught his finger between her teeth before catching his hand and pressing his palm to her moist lips, dropping it with a low guttural moan when he covered her mouth with his. Then there were more kisses, more caresses until her senses were singing.

She opened her eyes and looked up at his dark face above her and realised that she wanted him body and soul. She wanted him with a ferocity that scared her, feeling this much scared her. Emotion thickened her throat.

'You're so beautiful,' she whispered, trailing a hand down the damp skin of his chest and across the ridges of his flat belly, loving the texture, loving… With a little shake of her head she closed the avenue of thought and allowed her hand to slide lower, watching his eyes darken as her fingers closed around his shaft.

It wasn't just her touch that was torturing him, it was her big eyes wanting him, her big eyes touching a corner of his heart that had been in cold storage. Like blood returning to a frozen extremity, the sensation was pain, pleasure.

'Slow, remember,' he whispered against her mouth as he flipped her over to switch their positions. 'I want you to enjoy this. I want this to be special…' You deserve special, he thought, reminding himself that this was all new for her. And as he dug into patience and tenderness that he'd never known he possessed, it all felt new for him too.

'You are special, Zac.' She groaned as he slid an explosive hand between her legs.

He was the pure essence of all things male. Longing had stripped her of logic and pride and she writhed beneath the delicious torture of his clever carnal caresses as he devoted attention to every inch of her body.

It was Rose who, unable to bear another moment of the delicious torture, guided him between her legs, to feel him above her, inside her. The measured power of his thrusts drove her to a place where nothing existed beyond the two of them, their mingled gasps and moans, until the climax happened and she stopped breathing, just focused on everything that was happening inside her.

During the golden glow of the aftermath she lay with her head on his chest, her limbs weighed down by a soft lethargy until, finally summoning the energy, she lifted her head.

'Slow works for me.' As she curled up into him she missed the startled look on his face before he brought his arms around her.

Zac felt the moment her breathing changed and drew back to look at her sleeping face.

Her face lit by a light set in a stone embrasure above the bed, she looked a million miles from the wanton version of Rose, the uninhibited Rose who had matched him for passion. The sleeping Rose looked vulnerable, she looked as if she could break, which he knew was a lie. The woman he had made love to had been strong and fierce.

Were there any more Roses to discover?

She wouldn't be in his life long enough for him to find out. They were sharing a moment, not a life.

He could have retreated and taken refuge in his own bed—it was his normal modus operandi. Instead Zac switched off the light. He fell asleep smelling her hair.

CHAPTER TWELVE

WHEN ZAC WOKE up in the night he reached out groggily but found the bed beside him empty. He sat bolt upright and, without thinking, threw back the covers and swung his legs over the side, and as his feet hit the floor he heard a baby noise—noise as opposed to cry.

Pulling on the boxers he had taken off before he got into bed beside her, he headed to the nursery, and found the door open, the room lit by a rotating night light that threw illuminated animal shadows on the walls and ceiling.

Rose was standing in the middle of the room singing softly to the baby in her arms. As if she sensed his presence, her head lifted, her eyes widening as she saw him. She froze, then, after a moment of standing there transfixed, she glanced down at the baby before placing a finger to her lips in warning as her gaze returned to Zac.

He watched as she went over to the cot and laid her burden down before drawing the sheet up over him, and felt something shift and tighten in his chest. For several moments Zac forgot how to breathe.

She looked up, a question appearing in her eyes as their glances connected.

There was a tense silent beat.

This is just sex, Zac reminded himself.

On this perspective-establishing thought, he heard himself blurt stupidly, 'I like your perfume.'

He watched a confused groove appear in her smooth brow, which, given he sounded like some sort of tongue-tied teenage idiot, was not to be wondered at.

'I don't wear perfume,' she whispered back, glancing over her shoulder to check he hadn't woken the baby.

He turned and walked out of the room, glad of the sense-cooling moment before Rose joined him, carefully leaving the door ajar.

'Sorry to disturb you,' she whispered, her eyelids lowering on the memory of waking to find a heavy arm thrown across her hips… She had fully anticipated him waking as she'd eased herself away but he hadn't, he'd been deep asleep.

Disturb…she had no idea. He reached out and took her arm, just because he *needed* to touch her. It seemed thin beneath the long-sleeved nightdress she had pulled on, which had in its favour a virtual transparency under certain lighting conditions.

'You should have woken me.'

She had woken up next to a beautiful man, and thought he was a dream. She'd had to touch him to make sure he was real. The kiss had not been strictly necessary but she had been unable to resist the final reality check.

'What are you smiling at?' he asked suspiciously, observing the secret curve to her beautiful mouth. 'That is a very prim nightdress.'

'I'm sure Victorian misses got involved in some kissing when nobody was looking,' she retorted naughtily.

'Only the wicked ones,' he rasped, fitting his mouth to hers. She had read his intention but she still gasped at the contact, then groaned when the pressure deepened as his tongue slipped between her parted lips.

'Checking I've not been at the cooking sherry?' she whispered against his mouth.

'You don't taste of sherry, but you don't taste of me. I think we should work on that…'

Her heart was thudding like a drum. 'I d-don't know…' she faltered.

'Oh, I know… I know many things I think a wicked lady might enjoy, and I am a very good teacher.' She raised herself on tiptoe and linked her arms around his neck. 'Am I wicked?'

'With me you are deliciously wicked.' He glanced at the door. 'Is he likely to wake again?'

'It's always a possibility with a baby.'

'Then let us not waste time,' he said, matching his suggestion with action as he scooped her up in his arms and carried her back to the bedroom and the bed.

Much later she lay with her head on his damp chest listening to his heartbeat. His fingers were tangled in her hair.

'You are a g-good teacher,' she said, lifting her face from his chest and gazing at him through her lashes before she kissed his chin and burrowed back down against him.

'I hope Declan doesn't wake now.' She yawned.

He didn't, not until the morning and by then Zac had gone.

That morning set the pattern for the next ten days. Zac spent the nights with her but was gone by the time she woke. During the day Rose cared for Declan—at least it had begun that way but for the past few days Zac had broken into his working day and appeared at unexpected moments to spend a few minutes, an hour or even two with them. She admired the effort that he was making to bond with the baby. Yesterday Declan had slept the entire time he'd been with them and she had ruefully apologised, which had made him look at her... Yes, she decided, going over the moment in her head, it had been an *odd* look.

Maybe he'd read her thoughts?

The idea worried her, as her thoughts were embarrassingly foolish, because *this* wasn't what it felt like to be part of a family, because families were for ever, and this was...*for how long?*

With an effort she pushed away the question that would have spoilt the perfect moment if she'd allowed it space in her head.

All the effort in the world couldn't mask the fact she was a mass of quivering anticipation when he came to her each night. She didn't even try. What was the point? As much as she loved her days, she lived for her nights and the trembling anticipation was part of what she lived for!

And what would it feel like when the inevitable moment arrived and Zac didn't come to her bed? Sometimes she thought it might be easier if he lost interest now. Later would involve more devastation... whereas now...

Now it would hurt like hell!

Sometimes there was no upside to a situation that you walked into with your eyes wide open...everything wide open... Well, she wouldn't be the first woman to lose her heart to Zac Adamos, but she felt a wistful envy for the woman who was the last.

Today there had been no appearance of the tall figure who was fast becoming her drug of choice. It was early evening and Rose was taking advantage of Camille's presence in the nursery to explore, when he did appear. She had headed for the beach, the sand still warm on her bare feet as she wandered along the shoreline, swinging her shoes in her hand as she waded out to meet a wave and then ran back, allowing it to chase her.

'Having fun?'

More than the top of her cut-offs got wet when she heard his voice. Studying him, she forgot to watch for a wave and it hit the backs of her legs, drenching her up to the waist.

Other than the tie that was hanging loose around his neck, he looked as though he had just stepped out of a board meeting—maybe he had. The only place they were on an equal footing was in bed. Elsewhere he was very much the boss.

'Do you ever take a holiday?' she wondered out loud.

His grin suddenly flashed and he looked a lot less boardroom and a lot more bedroom. 'If I was on holiday I'd be giving you that swimming lesson,' he remarked, taking off his jacket and slinging it one-handed over a shoulder.

'I told you, I really don't want a swimming lesson.'

'You think I'm not qualified? You don't trust me?'

Rose refused to react to the challenge in his eyes. He was treating this as a joke, which to her it wasn't.

'I know you are a very good teacher, and yes…I *do* trust you.' The realisation came with a rush of surprise.

'So are you scared?'

A lie would have worked but the truth threw him. 'I am.'

He frowned and looked as discomposed as she had ever seen him. 'You'd be perfectly safe with me,' he protested.

'It's not about *you*.' Rose was starting to get angry. He just didn't seem to get it—so she told him. 'When I was nine my dad, who thought *he* was a great teacher, threw me in a river. He was a fan of sink or swim. I sank. I didn't just choke a bit, I nearly drowned. The doctors said that the cold helped me—my body shut down so I didn't have brain damage despite being deprived of oxygen for so long—so if it's OK with you, I'll paddle.'

'I had no idea.' That she had almost died because of the actions of a reckless man whose job it was to care for her winded him like a blow to the solar plexus.

He thought about a world without Rose Hill in it and without warning felt an emptiness rise up in him so strong that for several moments he just saw blackness.

Zac looked so shocked that she immediately felt guilty for wheeling out the old story. It was something she'd never done before, and she really wished she hadn't now. She hated sounding like a victim. She'd heard her dad do it so often. He'd never accepted responsibility in his life.

'My dad never accepted that I was in serious danger, because I suppose that would have made him responsible and that is not a role my dad feels happy playing.' Caught out in any wrongdoing, he always became the victim.

Zac's frown deepened. It would seem Rose had no illusions about her father, she knew what he was and he knew she was nothing like him, information he would have relayed to Marco had the man been able to say anything beyond a strained, *'Sorry. Later. Kate is in labour.'*

'Dad embroidered the story over the years, making it a big joke—I jumped in, I played the drama queen, and so on. So you hit a nerve. Can we talk about something else?' she asked, dropping her gaze. The pity she imagined she saw in his eyes made her feel uncomfortable. 'Did you pick up your messages? You had one from your father...' She stopped dead, realising that her awkward change of subject had left her sounding like an eavesdropper—which she was. 'The door to your study was open and the answer machine kicked in. Sorry, I shouldn't have listened, but I did.'

He arched a brow and looked amused by her faltering explanation and guilty admission. 'I had no mobile signal but he caught me later. He did mention he'd tried the landline.'

'A family party sounds lovely.'

Three weeks' time. Where will I be...?

She pushed the thought away and reminded herself that she was going to live in the moment. She flashed a covert glance up at his perfect profile and felt her tummy muscles quiver. The problem was she wanted the moment to last for ever. 'You'll be able to introduce Declan to his cousins,' she added brightly.

'I am not free.' He paused, the sea breeze ruffling his hair as he watched the animated approval fade from her face. She really didn't have a mouth made for compressing, he decided, staring at the full lush outline he had been thinking of all day. His focus had been shot to hell lately. A woman had never distracted him like this before in his life, but then he had never wanted a woman the way he wanted Rose.

'Oh, I just assumed that you'd want to introduce Declan to his family. Sorry, it's none of my business.'

He didn't contradict her. A *sensible* response to his closed expression would have been to drop the subject, but the emotions tightening like a fist in her chest would not be contained. They just spilled out.

'You have no idea how lucky you are. You have a family who love you, who want to be part of your life!' she yelled and saw the shock move across his face. 'And you push them away, at every turn you push them away!' she condemned. 'Well, fine, that's your choice, but this is about Declan and he will benefit from an extended family.' Zac's jaw had taken on an uncompromising angle, which vanished at her last quivering, 'He never needs to feel l-lonely.'

'Were you a lonely child?' he asked, things squeezing in his chest as he imagined her alone—the idea hurt.

Her eyes slid from his as she hid behind her lashes, her shrug saying, *If I have issues, they are mine*—an attitude that should have pleased him. Instead her stubborn self-reliance caused the protective walls he had spent a lifetime building around his emotions, dividing them into neat compartments, to crumble.

He wanted to share her pain, he wanted to take it away.

'You can be lonely in a room full of people.'

Zac recognised the avoidance and the truth of her

words. He had frequently felt lonely in the midst of his loving, noisy family, which was in part why he avoided putting himself in that situation.

'That is not answering my question.'

'What quest—' she began, then met his look and gave a resigned sigh. 'All right, maybe, but no more than any other only child. We moved around a lot. It was hard to make friends.' She turned back to him, shading her eyes from the evening sun but unable to read his face, her efforts frustrated when he stepped in close.

She stood still, fighting the urge to put her head against his chest, craving the physical contact, the illusion of safety it offered.

Was it an illusion? she wondered, remembering her unthinking response when he had asked if she trusted him, and she did. Becoming his lover had not been a decision she had questioned, any more than she would have questioned a tidal current. The feelings he awoke in her were just as elemental and primal, but she realised that it would not have happened if she hadn't trusted him.

'I know about scars that are invisible...'

'I have no scars.'

He ignored her protest and framed her face with his big hands, capturing her eyes with his dark obsidian stare. 'Are they why I was your first lover?'

That he appeared to have tuned in on her own train of thought startled Rose. For a moment she considered denying it, instead she hid her unease behind a flippant retort.

'Well, I wasn't keeping myself pure for Mr Right.' He didn't react to her weak laughter, which trailed away in the face of his stare. 'OK, my dad is a very convincing liar.' She took a step back and his hands fell away. She immediately missed the warmth. 'So I suppose,' she conceded, 'I do have a few trust issues.'

Watching her bare toes tracing swirls in the sand, she missed the expression that spread across his face.

The implication of her words was she trusted him, the irony not lost on Zac, who had been lying, at least by omission, from the outset, and now...

Is she the only person you're lying to, Zac?

He was able to switch off the inner dialogue but not the guilt, which remained like a sour aftertaste in his mouth. He tried and failed to spin his actions. Doing it for a friend just didn't cut it, especially when that friend would definitely have issues with Zac's own interpretation of the role he had been given.

He might be selfish, actually there was no might about it, and he rarely chose the option that was not in his best interest, an acknowledgment that did not make him proud. He could keep her in ignorance and keep her here in his bed. The logic was inescapable, or it might once have seemed that way.

The simple fact was she deserved to know that she had the family she craved for. He didn't have the right to deny her that and neither did Marco.

His plan was to tell her before he reported back to Marco. He owed her that much. The sooner this farce was brought to an end, the better as far as he was concerned.

It would be a very short report, basically because there wasn't one. There was nothing to report on except to say that with Rose Hill what you saw was what you got.

His one indulgence before he came clean was seeing her in a setting he had imagined her in, no longer looking the poor twin. She deserved to have the luxury that her sister enjoyed, and tomorrow she would.

Then he would do the big reveal. He could not predict her reaction, but he was pretty sure it would involve her leaving—which he told himself was a good thing. Perhaps she'd take this new and very uncomfortable conscience he had developed away with her. What would he miss, a few extra days, even weeks of incredible sex? He knew himself well enough to know that this attraction he felt would fade, hard to justify depriving her of a future with a family.

'There is a dinner and I'd like you to be the hostess.'

She stopped digging grooves in the sand and looked up, startled.

'I'm sure Arthur is much more capable than me at the list ticking and meet-and-greet stuff. I'm quite likely to send people home with the wrong coats.'

'I think you have the wrong idea. I don't want you to *take coats*! You will be there as my hostess for the evening, and with that in mind I have had Arthur send some appropriate clothing items to our room. Hopefully there will be something you like.'

'*Our* room?'

'All right, your room.' He held up a hand and cut

off further protest before she articulated it. 'Let me save you the effort: I will not take clothes from you, I have everything I need…blah…blah…' he drawled, sounding bored.

'Don't put words in my mouth.'

Zac struggled to string the words together as he stared at the lips under discussion and he wasn't thinking words!

'Tell me I am wrong, then,' he suggested. 'And in response to that I will say, no, you do not have anything suitable for a black-tie event and, secondly, it is nothing more than a uniform.'

'Meaning this is nothing more than a job?' She wished the words unsaid even before they left her lips but they seemed to have acquired a resentful will of their own.

'Now who is putting words in someone else's mouth?' he taunted, arching a satiric brow. 'I really don't get why you are being so pedantic, but for the record I am not asking Declan's nanny to be my hostess, I am asking a beautiful woman who shares my bed to be my partner for this dinner. So will you oblige me by doing this? It is a small event, twenty couples or so. I was intending to hold the reception in London, but circumstances intervened…'

So he'd had a date lined up and she was a last-minute stand-in. The possibility was not exactly ego-enhancing.

'What would I have to do?'

'Eat food, drink wine, make conversation and be agreeable. It should not be too taxing.'

Unless you were a social liability… Her dad's description of her floated into her head. She had never questioned his statement, let alone challenged it. She was ashamed that she had lacked the strength and just accepted it. It suddenly occurred to her that this was an opportunity to do just that, prove her dad wrong. He would never know but she would. Suddenly that was very important to Rose as she acknowledged a deep-buried truth, a *hurt* that she had carried.

Zac watched the emotions flicker across her face, saw the change in the tilt of her chin and the defiant resolution that put a sparkle in her eyes, and wondered about what had put it there.

His jaw tightened. It was not his business to wonder what belonged to the family she was about to gain. Before long she would be part of a royal household, protected and loved, and they were about to gain Rose, which made them the winner by any measurement he could think of in this equation.

'Fine, I'll do it, but anything I wear I'll…' Pay? Considering the sad state of her finances, that might prove difficult. 'You can take the cost out of my first pay cheque.'

'I will invoice you,' he responded seamlessly, seeing no reason to share the information that it would take more than one pay cheque to cover the cost of any of the items that he had signed off on.

'Good.'

'Excellent,' he returned, realising he had never

had to work so hard to have any woman fall in with his plans. Rose was damned hard work.

His heavy-lidded glance slid to her mouth—maybe she was worth some hard work. He pushed the thought away as with it came the temptation to ignore his conscience and keep her with him, keep Marco in the dark for a little longer.

'What exactly do I have to do at this dinner?'

'Make people feel at ease.'

What about me? Who puts me at my ease?

'How am I meant to do that?'

'People like to talk about themselves. Be interested, and…' He hesitated, the underlying amusement draining from his voice as he finished on advice he would offer few people. But then few people possessed Rose's natural warmth or her smile, and the fact she seemed utterly unaware of her power made it all the more effective. 'Be yourself, Rose.'

CHAPTER THIRTEEN

THE GUESTS, IT SEEMED, were not staying at the villa but, as Arthur explained, were being ferried in from Athens via helicopter and then flown back. Armed with the information that there were thirty guests and Camille's flattering opinion of her outfit, Rose went to join Zac, who, she had been informed, was waiting for her in the library.

She fingered the necklace that out of the selection had matched the dress she had chosen to wear, a bias-cut slip in a misty green with shoestring straps and a cowl neckline that just hinted at the swell of her breasts. If those stones had been real emeralds they would have been worth a small fortune. She wondered if people who walked around with a fortune around their necks felt nervous. But that wasn't a problem she would ever have, she reflected, smiling at the crazy thought.

She paused for a moment outside the door, telling herself that this was not about proving anything to her father or Zac or anyone else, this was about her. She was doing this for herself.

She walked in without knocking and Zac, who had been standing looking out of the window, turned around. Her breath caught in her throat as she made a rapid toe-to-head survey of his long, lean, lithe body looking utterly spectacular in a formal black-tie dress suit. He looked scarily beautiful and she had no control over her physical reaction to him. Hopefully she retained come control over her facial expression, but she doubted she did.

He had wanted the indulgence of seeing her in the sort of clothes she deserved to wear and now he was. The image of her standing there, the green dress clinging to her supple curves, the jewels around her white throat that needed no adornment, her glorious hair pinned in a loose knot at the nape of her neck, made him want to undo the pins and watch her shake it loose down her slender back.

She deserved the truth, but it would take her from him… He tried to distance himself from the internal battle raging in his head. She would hate him either way.

'You look very beautiful.'

His own voice sounded distant and stiff in Zac's ears as he pushed out the words above the flames licking through his body. Only the guilt gnawing through him stopped him from pulling those pins out of her hair and watching it slip like silk down her back.

Her skin prickled with heat, even her scalp took part in the nerve-tingling assault on her senses. She wanted to tell him how she felt. One look or word from him would have given her the courage, but his air of remoteness made her feel stupid for wanting to declare her feelings and invite rejection.

She pinned on an overbright smile. 'I'm looking forward to this evening,' she lied. She was actually wondering what she was trying to prove. This thing, whatever it was, was going to end badly—did it really matter if that end came tonight or another night? she asked herself bleakly.

When they walked into the room where a string quartet were playing and the guests, glasses in hand, chatted in front of French doors that had been flung open, all eyes turned their way.

Rose froze like someone caught in a spotlight, only moving when she felt the light comforting pressure of Zac's hand in the small of her back.

He watched proudly as she overcame her fears and gradually relaxed as she conversed with the guests, people drawn by her smile and the beauty she was unaware of. By the time they had sat down at the table for the meal she seemed totally at ease.

Except he knew she wasn't. He could see the tension in her shoulders, the tautness in the lovely line of her neck that showed the emerald choker he had noticed in an online auction and had immediately wanted to see against her glowing skin.

Rose knew it was going well and she only wished she could enjoy her success, but she didn't want to be here. She wanted to be anywhere alone with Zac… She'd always dreamed of a home of her own but now she knew that it wasn't about a place, but a person, and the person who was her home just wanted sex. He had a history of keeping everyone, even his closest family, at a distance, and despite her determination to enjoy the moments she had and extract every ounce of pleasure from being with him it was spoilt by thoughts of the future—a future that was never going to include Zac.

The effort of maintaining a front was exhausting, and by the time the only guest remaining was the guest of honour himself, who Zac personally escorted to the waiting helicopter, Rose felt drained.

'A nightcap in the library,' Zac suggested as he walked away. Something in his voice planted the conviction in her head that this would be more than a nightcap, and once the notion that this was goodbye took root, she couldn't shake it.

She walked alone to the library. She would be dignified, she had decided, she would not break down or say something stupid. While she waited, pacing the book-lined room, she caught a glass vase with her elbow. She spun and caught it before it smashed but in the process knocked against a sleeping laptop that surged into life.

Clutching the vase, she turned and her glance landed on the image and headline that appeared on the screen.

The new Princess!

Crown Prince Marco Zanetti of Renzoi married today in the island's cathedral, watched by guests including European royalty and many A-listers, including his good friend, the Greek billionaire, Zac Adamos.

Rose read the paragraph three times, her eyes moving between the new royal couple and Zac, looking urbane and utterly gorgeous…but the face that she kept going back to was that of the princess, because it was her own face. Someone else was wearing her face, a stranger was wearing her face, and Zac was there.

Zac walked into the room, saw the image on the screen and knew it was too late.

Rose, her face as pale as milk, turned when he entered.

'Who is she?'

'Your twin sister. Your father refused to take her back when your mother died, and she was adopted.'

'A sister…a twin?'

'She wanted you both, she loved you both,' Zac said, solemnly.

'My mother didn't leave me? I have a family?' Her eyes zeroed in on his face. 'And you knew?' She shook her head. 'I don't understand…' But she did. Not all of it but most of it, and she could feel the anger surging through her at the betrayal he had compounded.

Zac dragged a hand down his jaw. 'It's not what it appears.'

'Isn't it? Then what is it? You knew who I was from the start?'

His slow nod confirmed her worst fears and the

sense of betrayal lodged in her chest felt like a boulder. 'You knew and you didn't tell me.' She breathed out in disbelief. 'None of this is accidental, is it? It was all some sort of set-up... What... I still don't understand, my sister is a part of this?' She felt as if she were choking on the hurt and humiliation. If her heart hadn't turned to stone it would have broken. Instead it was frozen.

'No...no. Kate was looking for you. She doesn't know that Marco, her husband, located you.'

Her sister, her twin, the one she didn't know she had, had been looking for her. Rose struggled to take in the bizarre facts.

'Look, I'm not the person who should be telling you this, but Kate was adopted. She didn't know that she had a twin, but she found a photo and—'

'What am I doing here? Why did this Marco not tell m-my *sister*?'

'Kate is pregnant and she's been unwell. Marco didn't want to upset her again, after your father—'

Her face between her hands, she let out a low keening sound. 'My dad knew... Why am I surprised? Am I the *only* person in the world who doesn't know? Unwell—you said unwell...?' She walked right up to him and grabbed the lapels of his jacket as though she'd shake the truth out him.

'Something to do with blood pressure, but she gave birth to a son yesterday. I just had a text.'

'Oh, that's...' she began releasing the fabric when she paused, her hands tightening into fists. 'You— where do you come in this...this charade? What part

do you play, Zac? I take it I'm not here by accident…'
Of course she wasn't. Why had she not clocked this
earlier? It had never really stood up to scrutiny, but
she hadn't scrutinised.

'Marco is my friend. He asked me…you understand. He wanted to know if you were like your…if
you were genuine or—'

'Like my father…and you were trying to catch
me out. Was sex part of the plan? Are you reporting
back on that too…grading me perhaps?' she wondered with withering scorn.

He winced and opened his hands in a pacifying
gesture. 'You, me, none of what happened between
us was meant to—' he began urgently, only to be
cut off by her yell.

'Stop…stop talking!' His agonised expression
only fed her fury. She was the one who had been
lied to and used, he was the one that did the lying
and she had trusted him, felt safe with him.

'I finally trusted someone and it was you—you!'
she repeated, her stabbing finger jabbing his chest.
She caught her head in her hands…the level of her
stupidity was just… 'Stupid, stupid, s-stupid!' she
cried, backing away from the hand he extended towards her.

'What can I do, Rose?'

'You can get me in touch with my sister and you
can whistle up one of your helicopters because I am
not spending another night under this roof!' she spat
at him disdainfully. 'And don't try to use Declan. It's
perfectly obvious that Camille is more than capable

of looking after him… You know, you made me love that little boy and I will n-never forgive you for that. At least I *can* love,' she added, looking him up and down with an expression of utter contempt. 'I don't know what your problem is, Zac, and I don't want to, but you cut yourself off, you deny yourself love… even your family you push away… One day they'll stop trying and then you'll really be alone!'

With a sob that tore his insides she turned and fled, not seeing the hand that Zac extended to her or the look of utter loss etched into his dark features.

Zac was still sitting in the chair he had slumped into when he heard the helicopter take off. Five minutes later Arthur appeared.

'She has gone?'

Zac said nothing.

The older man nodded. 'For what's it worth…my opinion…she was a keeper and you, boss, are a fool.'

The anger in Zac's eyes flared and died as Arthur held his gaze.

'Not for the first time.'

'This is different, boss.'

It was, Zac realised, because Rose had changed him…knowing and, yes, *loving* her had caused a shift in his mindset. He was not the person he had been even though he carried the same baggage. The difference was that now he knew that was *his* choice, he could have let it go, he could have lowered his protective barriers and let people in… And even if Rose wouldn't take him back, he would still do that.

Rose had woken him up.

And he had let her go!

'You're right, I am a fool.'

'That sounds like a good start.'

Rose had spent the long flight hating Zac and wanting to beg them to turn the plane around to get back to him in a miserable cycle. The inexplicable draw she felt to him was real and the farther she got away from him, the more she suffered a deep sense of deprivation.

She had been right. There were soulmates, people that you were drawn to against all logic, but she'd been wrong thinking that soulmate was a perfect partner.

The transfer was a blur and now, as she sat exhausted and dishevelled, feeling hollowed out, in an outer chamber of the palace on the island kingdom of Renzoi, she felt less scared than she would have imagined. The worst had already happened, so what was left to be afraid of?

Despite her alleged lack of fear, her knees were knocking. Rose went through all the possible outcomes that she had developed in her head—she was seeing her sister and this had been achieved in the space of twenty-four hours.

The telephone number that Arthur had given her on behalf of Zac—who at least had the sense not to try to stop her—had not put her through to some generic palace number or even the Crown Prince or one of his minions, but her sister in person.

Rose had just blurted, 'I'm your sister!' before she burst into sobs.

It would not have been surprising if her twin had hung up on her, but she hadn't, she'd stayed on the line until Rose was able to huskily continue.

As she'd listened to Rose's story she had responded with a level of anger equal to, if not exceeding, her own.

'I will kill Marco,' she declared, sounding as if she meant it. 'He has treated me like a child all the way through the pregnancy.'

Rose really didn't want Zac to get off so lightly. She had sobbed her way halfway around the world because of him and there was a massive empty space inside her that she felt would never be filled.

She had trusted him and he had betrayed her. 'But Zac—'

'Zac is a good friend and Marco took advantage, he put him, both of you, in a terrible position.' Her twin had seemed more dismissive of the part Zac played in the deception, saying that Marco had exploited the loyalty of his friend. It was a viewpoint that Rose had not previously considered.

A door opened and Rose looked up as a young man appeared, his eyes widening a little when he saw Rose, a reaction she had experienced several times since she arrived.

He introduced himself. 'I hope you had a good journey? The princess hadn't been told you had arrived. She was, er, feeding the baby,' he said, lowering his voice as though this information was sensitive. 'I have instructions to bring you right to her.'

Rose stepped with some trepidation into what was a sitting room. The moment her eyes met those of her mirror image, who had sprung to her feet, her doubts and fears melted away. They ran into each other's arms.

After the hugging and the tears came the cups of tea and the talking. There were so many things they had in common and so many experiences they yet had to share.

'So our mother died, she didn't reject me?'

'Is that what the old bastard told you?' the princess exclaimed. 'He came here and... I'm so very sorry that you were left with him. My adopted family...' She smiled. 'I can't wait for you to meet them.'

'I always wanted a family and I thought... I won't see Declan again!' Rose wailed.

Slowly the whole story emerged, relayed in shaky fits and starts as she was gently encouraged to get it all out by her sympathetic audience.

The exchange was interrupted when a tall, extremely handsome man appeared.

The prince addressed Rose, not his wife.

'I must apologise. My only defence is my intentions were good, but,' he added quickly in response to the snort from his wife, 'I have been told that I am guilty of infantilising grown women who are able to make their own choices.' He flashed a look at his wife, who Rose could see was fighting off a smile. 'Is that not right?'

There was another snort but Rose could tell her twin's anger was feigned now. 'Do not think you are forgiven yet.'

'You will let me know when I can stop grovelling?' He halted at the arrival of another snort and moved swiftly on. 'Zac is here. He is asking to see Rose. I told him—I told him that it was not my decision to make.'

This time Kate did not hide her grin. 'You're learning.' She turned to her twin. 'So will you see him?'

Rose's heart was hammering a frantic tattoo as it tried to climb out of her chest. 'No…yes…maybe… I think…'

She gazed around the room on the point of tipping over into panic when her twin clasped her arm, pulling her into a hug, and took the decision out of her hands. 'Tell him to come up, Marco,' she said quietly.

'I doubt I could stop him if I tried.'

'Rose, I'll leave. Later you can meet your nephew and his big sister.'

Left alone, Rose began to pace, wringing her hands. Zac was here…why? What did that mean? The door opened and she stopped, her eyes drinking him in… From the beginnings of a beard on his jaw, it would appear he had not shaved since she last saw him, the haggard look around his gorgeous eyes suggested he hadn't had much sleep either, but then that made two of them.

'Thank you for seeing me,' he said, devouring her with his dark-ringed eyes.

Rose didn't say anything. She couldn't. Her throat was clogged with emotion.

'Will you allow me to…? Oh, to hell with this, I'll just say it.' He gave a fatalistic laugh and rushed into impetuous, passionate speech. 'You said I denied myself love, kept myself apart, and it is true I do that. I…I never wanted to hurt anyone…' She could not maintain her frosty stance in the face of his obvious anguish. The tortured expression in his dark eyes tore at her tender heart.

'Tell me, Zac,' she said softly. Whatever he was holding inside was eating him up.

'You know that Kairos, my mother's first husband, raised me. He has been good to me, more so than people understand. My father died of a drug overdose—he was a dealer and an abuser. When my mother, who was sixteen when she was with him, didn't have an abortion as he instructed, he tried to beat the baby, me, out of her… It didn't work and he was sent to prison for the assault, where another inmate stabbed him. When he was in the hospital wing he acquired drugs and overdosed.

'*That* is my heritage, that is the child that Kairos welcomed into his home. I even look like him, apparently, so my mother has to see her abuser every time—'

His voice cracked and she rushed to him, wrapping her arms around him as she buried her face against his chest. 'Your mother sees the son she loves, that is obvious from what you have said. She knows, your stepfather knows, that you are not responsible for your father's actions any more than I am responsible for mine.' She lifted her face to his. 'Unless you think I am?'

'Of course I don't!' he exclaimed, sounding offended by the suggestion as he framed her face between his big hands.

She smiled up at him. 'Exactly.'

'It's not the same. My father was violent, *vile*. If I hurt someone that I cared for…? That I loved…'

His naked fear was out there in the open and her heart ached for the secret dread he had kept inside.

'But you won't,' she said with utmost confidence. 'You are not a predator, you are the opposite. Please don't deny yourself love, Zac. I don't mean me… that is, I *do* love you, but I understand if you can't love me back,' she said, doing what she knew was a feeble job of sounding OK with the situation. 'There will be someone else and—'

'You love me?'

Her eyes slid from his so she missed the fire that lit them. 'Well, I would have thought it was obvious, but as you are being honest so will I. Yes, I'm crazy mad in love with you—'

She got no farther as he rained kisses on her face before claiming her lips and kissing her deeply, soul deep.

'I love you, Rose. The darkness I have carried inside me, you have shone a cleansing light on it. I swear I will never hurt you.'

'I have always felt safe with you, Zac,' she said, stroking his stubble-roughened cheek lovingly.

'You will want children. When I see you with Declan... I never thought I'd father a child, but a child with you...?'

She smiled, more happy than she had ever imagined she could be. 'Don't you think we should get married first?'

He drew back in mock shock, his eyes smiling down at her. 'Did you just propose to me?'

'I rather think I did.'

'Then, my dearest love, my only love, the answer is yes!'

* * * * *

Enchanted by
Her Forbidden Awakening in Greece?
Then catch the first instalment in
The Secret Twin Sisters duet

The Prince's Forbidden Cinderella

Also don't miss the drama of these other stories
by Kim Lawrence!

Claiming His Unknown Son
Waking Up in His Royal Bed
The Italian's Bride on Paper
Innocent in the Sicilian's Palazzo
Claimed by Her Greek Boss

Available now!

#4137 NINE MONTHS TO SAVE THEIR MARRIAGE
by Annie West

After his business-deal wife leaves, Jack is intent on getting their on-paper union back on track. He just never imagined their reunion would be *scorching*. Or that their red-hot Caribbean nights would leave Bess *pregnant*! Is this their chance to finally find happiness?

#4138 PREGNANT WITH HER ROYAL BOSS'S BABY
Three Ruthless Kings
by Jackie Ashenden

King Augustine may rule a kingdom, but loyal assistant Freddie runs his calendar. There's no task she can't handle. Except perhaps having to tell her boss she's going to need some time off...because in six months she'll be having *his* heir!

#4139 THE SPANIARD'S LAST-MINUTE WIFE
Innocent Stolen Brides
by Caitlin Crews

Sneaking into ruthless Spaniard Lionel's wedding ceremony, Geraldine arrives just in time to see him being jilted. But Lionel is still in need of a convenient wife...and innocent Geraldine suddenly finds *herself* being led to the altar!

#4140 A VIRGIN FOR THE DESERT KING
The Royal Desert Legacy
by Maisey Yates

After years spent as a political prisoner, Sheikh Riyaz has been released. Now it's Brianna's job to prepare him for his long-arranged royal wedding. But the forbidden attraction flaming between them tempts her to cast duty—and her *innocence*!—to the desert winds...

HPCNMRA0823

#4141 REDEEMED BY MY FORBIDDEN HOUSEKEEPER
by Heidi Rice

Recovering from a near-deadly accident, playboy Renzo retreated to his Côte d'Azur estate. Nothing breaks through his solitude. Until the arrival of his new yet strangely familiar housekeeper, Jessie, stirs dormant desires...

#4142 HIS JET-SET NIGHTS WITH THE INNOCENT
by Pippa Roscoe

When archaeologist Evelyn needs his help saving her professional reputation, Mateo reluctantly agrees. Only the billionaire hadn't bargained on a quest around the world... From Spain to Shanghai, each city holds a different adventure. Yet one thing is constant: their intoxicating attraction!

#4143 HOW THE ITALIAN CLAIMED HER
by Jennifer Hayward

To save his failing fashion house, CEO Cristiano needs the face of the brand, Jensen, to clean up her headline-hitting reputation. But while she's lying low at his Lake Como estate, he's caught between his company...and his desire for the scandalous supermodel!

#4144 AN HEIR FOR THE VENGEFUL BILLIONAIRE
by Rosie Maxwell

Memories of his passion-fueled night with Carrie consume tycoon Damon. Until he discovers the ugly past that connects them and pledges to erase every memory of her. Then she storms into his office...and announces she's carrying his child!

YOU CAN FIND MORE INFORMATION ON UPCOMING HARLEQUIN TITLES, FREE EXCERPTS AND MORE AT HARLEQUIN.COM.

HPCNMRB0823

HARLEQUIN
PLUS

Try the best multimedia subscription service for romance readers like you!

Read, Watch and Play.

Experience the easiest way to get the romance content you crave.

Start your **FREE TRIAL** at
www.harlequinplus.com/freetrial.